NATIONAL PARKS
HISTORY OF THE WPA POSTER ART

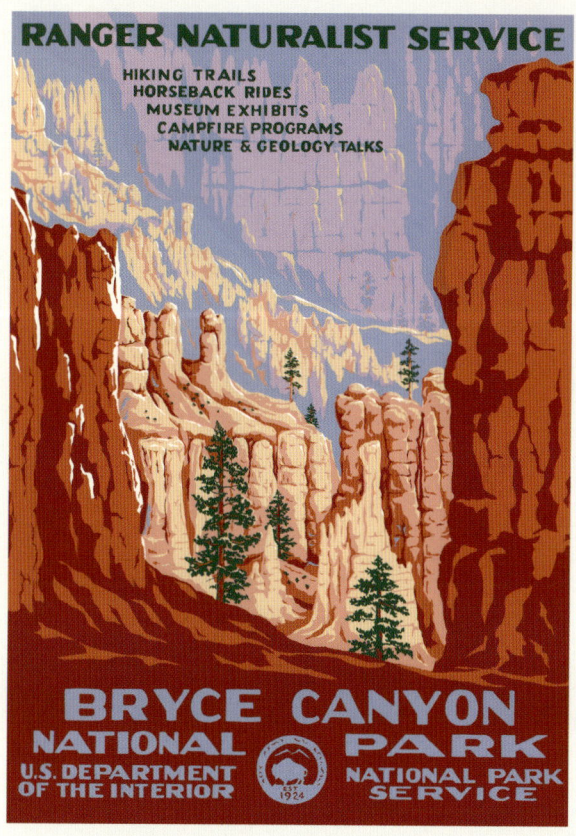

Deborah T. Zindell
Jeanne-Marie P. Hudson

Introduction by Doug Leen

National Parks—History of the WPA Poster Art is published by Ziga Media, LLC
© 2017 Ziga Media, LLC
5 Overbrook Lane, Darien, CT 06820
203.656.0076

zigamedia.com [f] [o] ZigaMedia

Printed in China
ISBN: 978-1-61983-654-9
2018 2019 2020 / 10 9 8 7 6 5 4 3 2

All color poster images © *Ranger Doug's Enterprises*
Other sources:
Page 5: Western Museum Laboratories, *John GInno Aronovici*
Page 6: Chester Don Powell with his screener Dale Miller, *Richard & Nancy Powell*
Page 7: 1940 Park Display, *National Park Service*
Page 23: Lassen Volcanic National Park poster inset, *Prints and Photographs
Division/Library of Congress*
Page 37: Zion National Park poster inset, *Prints and Photographs Division/
Library of Congress*

These images are available in the original poster format and also as
notecards and postcards from most National Park bookstores or from
Ranger Doug's Enterprises, 25 Nickerson Street, Seattle, WA 98109
Phone: (888) WPA POSTers (888-972-7678) and on the web at www.rangerdoug.com

For National Park WPA journals, calendars, and puzzles go to zigamedia.com

CONTENTS

REDISCOVERY, RE-PUBLICATION, AND RE-EMERGENCE OF THE WPA NATIONAL PARK POSTERS

After the stock market crash of 1929 and the subsequent economic depression, President Franklin D. Roosevelt launched a massive bureaucratic structure called the New Deal whose primary goal was to put America back to work. Between 1935 and 1943, the WPA, or Works Progress Administration (later renamed Work Projects Administration), was established by presidential order and employed more than 8 million workers. Seven percent of the WPA budget went for arts projects, producing 475,000 artworks through the Federal Writers' Project, the Federal Theatre Project, the Federal Music Project, and the Federal Art Project.

The efforts of the Federal Art Project are mainly known today by the 4,000 public murals that survive on the walls of schools, hospitals, and other public buildings. Perhaps least known, by virtue of the fragile nature of paper and cardboard, are the more than 2 million posters that were printed by the Federal Art Project's poster division. These posters were based on 35,000 designs, of which approximately 2,000 posters survive today. Sadly, nearly 33,000 poster designs have been lost forever, representing 99.9 percent of our public poster art.

The early posters were individually hand-painted in one or two colors and were produced in very limited quantities. Poster subjects included art, theater, travel, education, health, and safety. Initially, about a third of the artists producing these posters resided in New York City; however, by 1938 the WPA/FAP poster divisions had spread to all 48 states, with the Chicago units producing as many as 1,500 posters per day—in up to eight colors— for as little as 10 cents a poster. This prolific output was largely due to Anthony Velonis and his implementation of the silkscreen process.

LEFT: The Western Museum Laboratories produced interpretive materials and museum exhibits for the National Park Service.

On August 26, 1938, the National Park Service poster program was launched by Dorr Yeager, assistant chief of the Museum Division of the Western Museum Laboratories in Berkeley, California, using WPA artists. In his letter to Frank Pinkley, Superintendent at Southwestern Monuments in Coolidge, Arizona, Yeager clearly adopted the improved silkscreen techniques of Anthony Velonis. Accompanying this letter were 10 poster designs, which included a preliminary sketch for Grand Teton National Park. In this letter Yeager stated:

> This poster for Grand Teton was made up more or less as an experiment and does not in any way represent the best which can be obtained by the process. Future posters, especially the lettering, will be of a much higher standard.

This "Jenny Lake Museum" poster stands alone in its styling and lettering, harkening to earlier stylized WPA poster designs. From Yellowstone geyser (believed to be the second publication) onward, most posters featured the "Ranger Naturalist Service" banner at the top with more literal graphic interpretations of National Park scenes.

WPA artist Chester Don Powell was probably the chief designer of the "Ranger Naturalist" series. Only 14 National Park designs were produced, ending in 1941 with Bandelier National Monument. The number of posters

LEFT: WPA artist Chester Don Powell and his screener Dale Miller at the Western Regional Laboratories, Berkeley, California, c. 1938.

OPPOSITE: The 1940 display introducing the National Park WPA poster project.

printed of each design is unknown, but the fragility of silkscreens used at this time would have limited each edition to between 50 and 100 posters. Posters cost $12 per hundred or just 12 cents each. They were most likely produced and distributed to local Chambers of Commerce in communities surrounding each park to encourage visitation. At the close of publication in 1941, the remnants of this park collection were distributed back to the parks.

For 35 years, they disappeared into history. Then, in 1973, a Grand Teton poster turned up destined for the park burn-pile. It was this poster that piqued the curiosity of seasonal park ranger Doug Leen, and a 20-year effort led him to Harpers Ferry, West Virginia, where 13 black-and-white negatives survived in the file drawers of the National Park Service archives. These negatives and the single poster, then the only one known to survive, were the templates used for reconstruction of this set.

With the re-publication efforts under way, originals slowly began to emerge back into the public domain. It took another five years for two Mount Rainier posters to surface in a garage near Seattle, rescued in a similar fashion from under a park log cabin. A year later, another Mount Rainier poster turned up in an original frame. When taken apart to clean the glass, it was discovered that three posters were "sandwiched" together— the center one in pristine condition. These original colors were used for a limited edition for Mount Rainier's Centennial, celebrated in 1999, and the other two were donated back to the National Park Service.

National Parks started searching their archives' flat files, with Grand Canyon and Petrified Forest finding originals stashed away. The Petrified Forest National Monument poster boasted a full nine colors! In 2003 Bandelier National Monument discovered 13 posters in a file drawer— some cut up and used as cardboard file dividers! In 2004 a Los Angeles art collector stumbled upon the largest single find: nine original park posters, which later sold at auction, the Grand Canyon poster bringing $9,000—the first test of value in a free market. And in 2007, a third Grand Teton poster surfaced as cardboard in a plant press in White Sands, New Mexico. Today, 42 originals have been found, with only one copy each for Yosemite, Yellowstone Falls, and Petrified Forest. The two posters that remain unaccounted for are Wind Cave and Great Smoky Mountains.

Because only 14 parks subscribed to the Western Museum Laboratory's 1938 offer to produce posters, many parks today have commissioned contemporary images "in the style of" the WPA, the first in 1997 of Devils Tower. This was followed by Bryce Canyon, Mt. McKinley (now Denali), Olympic, Mesa Verde, Hawai'i (now Hawai'i Volcanoes), Rocky Mountain, and many others. These designs are a collaborative effort by both Doug Leen and Brian Maebius, with more park designs in progress. Recoloration of the historic reproductions has been formulated from analysis of the black-and-white photos as well as comparison with period art for each geographic area.

—Doug Leen

HISTORIC WPA NATIONAL PARK POSTERS

*Who will gainsay that the parks contain the highest
potentialities of national pride, national contentment,
and national health? A visit inspires love of country;
begets contentment; engenders pride of possession;
contains the antidote for national restlessness . . .
He is a better citizen with a keener appreciation of the
privilege of living here who has toured the national parks.*

— Stephen T. Mather
NPS Director, 1917–29

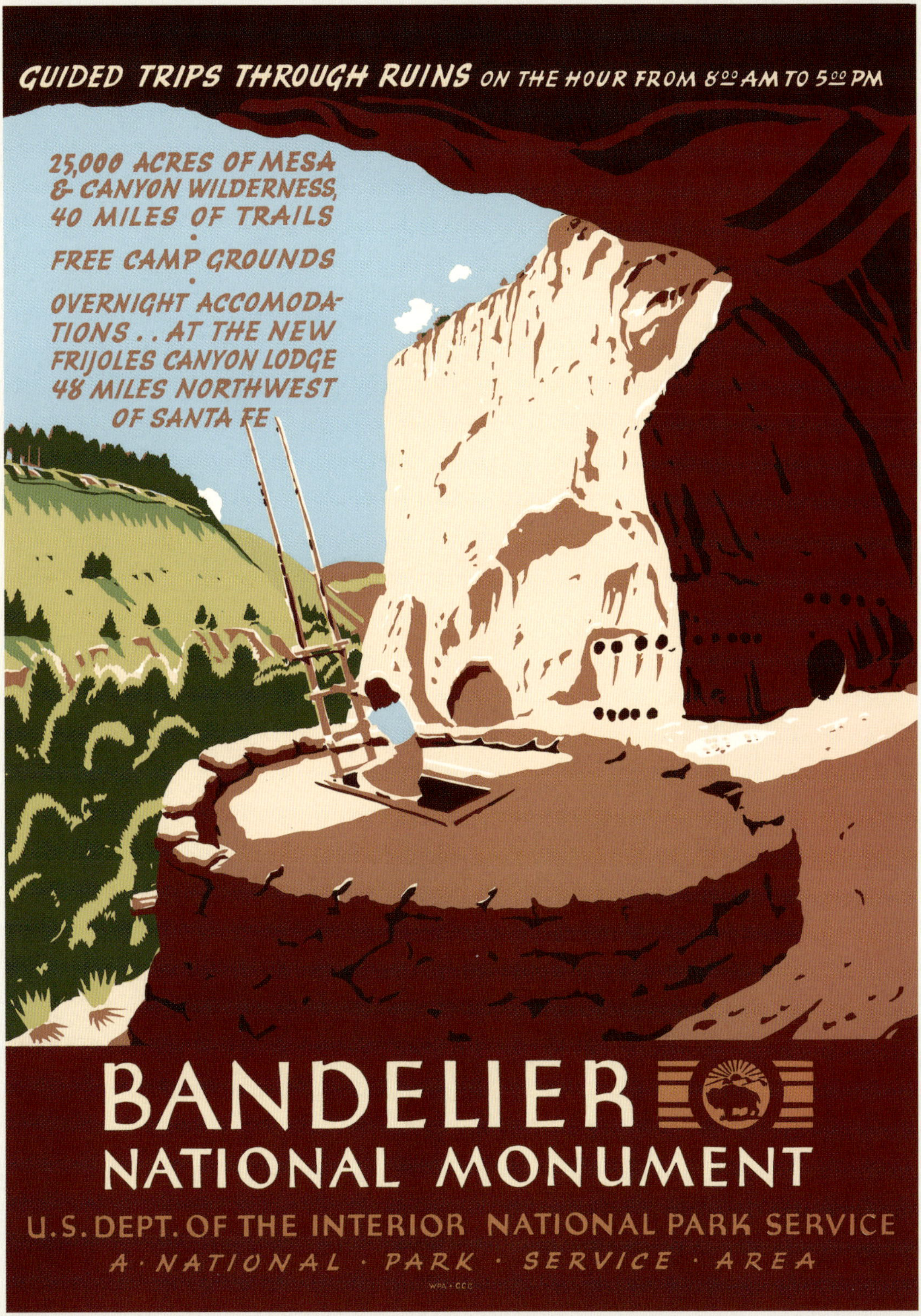

GUIDED TRIPS THROUGH RUINS ON THE HOUR FROM 8ºº AM TO 5ºº PM

25,000 ACRES OF MESA
& CANYON WILDERNESS,
40 MILES OF TRAILS
·
FREE CAMP GROUNDS
·
OVERNIGHT ACCOMODA-
TIONS .. AT THE NEW
FRIJOLES CANYON LODGE
48 MILES NORTHWEST
OF SANTA FE

BANDELIER
NATIONAL MONUMENT

U.S. DEPT. OF THE INTERIOR NATIONAL PARK SERVICE

A · NATIONAL · PARK · SERVICE · AREA

WPA · CCC

BANDELIER N.M.

New Mexico
Est. February 11, 1916
33,677 acres (13,628 ha)

The American Indian is of the soil, whether it be the region of forests, plains, pueblos, or mesas. He fits into the landscape, for the hand that fashioned the continent also fashioned the man for his surroundings.

—Luther Standing Bear

Bandelier National Monument occupies the southern edge of the Pajarito Plateau, which was created by volcanic eruptions over a million years ago. The result is a land of rugged but stunning beauty, where the elevation gradient ranges from 5,340 feet (1,627 m) at the Rio Grande to 10,199 feet (3,108 m) at Cerro Grande's summit—over a distance just shy of 12 miles (19 km). This varied terrain—from woodland, ponderosa pine savannah, and conifer forest to grassland, montane meadow, and wetland—provided favorable conditions for supporting the Ancestral Puebloan people from around A.D. 1150–1550. Severe drought may have caused this thriving culture to abandon their homes, leaving behind ample evidence of their existence, including cave dwellings carved into the volcanic tuff, petroglyphs, and standing masonry walls.

The Bandelier National Monument poster, the last of the 14 posters published by the park service WPA artists in Berkeley, California, depicts a visitor descending into a kiva, a chamber used by male Pueblo Indians for religious ceremonies. Frijoles Canyon Lodge, mentioned on the poster and built with native stone, still offers comfortable accommodations from May to October and remains one of the most authentically charming resorts in the Santa Fe area.

UNITED STATES DEPARTMENT OF THE INTERIOR
NATIONAL PARK SERVICE

FORT MARION
NATIONAL MONUMENT
ST. AUGUSTINE, FLORIDA

EST 1924

CASTILLO DE SAN MARCOS N.M.

Florida
Est. 1924 (Fort Marion N.M.)
20.5 acres (8.3 ha)

There is nothing that strengthens a nation like reading of a nation's own history, whether that history is recorded in books or embodied in customs, institutions, and monuments.

—Joseph Anderson

Fort Marion was designated a National Monument in 1924, and became a historic property of the National Park Service upon its transfer from the War Department in 1933. In 1942, Congress authorized the site to be officially renamed Castillo de San Marcos in recognition of its Spanish heritage.

Castillo de San Marcos claims the distinction of being the oldest permanent seacoast fort in the continental U.S. Constructed between 1682 and 1756 to defend Spanish holdings in Florida and the shipping lanes off the Florida coast, the fortification played a role in the colonial conflict between Great Britain and Spain in the 17th–18th centuries, billeted the British during the American Revolution, and served as an American bastion during the Spanish-American War.

The fort's architecture is significant, as it is the only existing 17th-century fort in North America, and the oldest masonry fort in the continental U.S. Its distinctive star-shaped construction follows the "bastion system," developed in 15th-century Italy.

The Fort Marion poster highlights the monument's history as an enduring symbol of our nation's complex cultural past. The serigraph follows the historic design and colors, except for the orange brick motif, which represents coquina bricks, made from rock containing tiny clam shells abundant on northeast Florida beaches.

RANGER NATURALIST SERVICE

FIELD TRIPS—CAMPFIRE PROGRAMS
NATURAL HISTORY TALKS & DISPLAYS
GENERAL INFORMATION

GLACIER
NATIONAL   PARK

U.S. DEPARTMENT
OF THE INTERIOR

EST.
1910

NATIONAL PARK
SERVICE

GLACIER N.P.

Montana
Est. May 11, 1910
1,013,322 acres (410,077 ha)

Far away in Montana, hidden from view by clustering mountain-peaks, lies an unmapped northwestern corner—the Crown of the Continent. The water from the crusted snowdrift which caps the peak of a lofty mountain there trickles into tiny rills . . . growing to rivers, [which] at last pour their currents into three seas . . . Here is a land of striking scenery.

—George Bird Grinnell

Boasting one of the largest and most intact swaths of wilderness in North America, Glacier National Park, in the Northern Rocky Mountains, is comprised of over one million acres of untamed, untouched natural landscapes. Although the rugged environment still requires those who venture into it to possess qualities of persistence and endurance, evidence of human habitation here dates back some 10,000 years. Ninety-three percent of the park is designated wilderness, but more than 740 miles (1,191 km) of maintained trails beckon hikers to its pristine lakes, alpine meadows, chiseled peaks, and ancient glaciers. The 50-mile (80 km) Going-to-the-Sun Road is one of the park's most popular visitor-friendly attractions, affording vehicular traffic stunning vistas and wildlife viewing.

Part of the original WPA poster project, this Glacier artwork was re-created here from archived black-and-white negatives. The poster shows Mount Gould above Swiftcurrent Lake on the east side of the park. Two original posters are in private collections, one of the prints curiously differing in design by the omission of the text field below the banner. The original colors include a yellow sky.

A FREE GOVERNMENT SERVICE
GRAND CANYON
NATIONAL PARK
U.S. DEPARTMENT
OF THE INTERIOR

EST 1919

NATIONAL PARK
SERVICE

GRAND CANYON N.P.

Arizona
Est. February 26, 1919
1,217,403 acres (487,350 ha)

The glories and the beauties of form, color, and sound unite in the Grand Canyon—forms unrivaled even by the mountains, colors that vie with sunsets, and sounds that span the diapason from tempest to tinkling raindrop, from cataract to bubbling fountain.
—John Wesley Powell

Even on the clearest day at Grand Canyon National Park, when visibility is between 90 and 110 miles (145–177 km), only a portion of the immense gorge can be seen from any single vantage point. Spearheaded by Theodore Roosevelt, Grand Canyon National Game Reserve was established in 1906; the area became a national monument two years later, and received National Park status in 1919. The Grand Canyon is one of the world's most breathtaking landscapes, carved by the Colorado River and its tributaries over the course of 6 million years. Close to 5 million people visit the canyon each year, most of them taking in the view from the South Rim, where the grand panorama presents an impressive sampling of the geologic features that exist throughout the canyon, citadels of stone that have inspired such lofty names as *temple*, *castle*, *altar*, and *spire*.

The poster announcing the "Free Government Service, Grand Canyon National Park" was one of the original in the WPA poster series. Re-created from archived negatives, with its colors based on an original poster that announced "Ranger Naturalist Service," the poster's depiction of the river and the cliff features in the distance indicate that the WPA artists most likely made their sketches for the Grand Canyon poster from Moran Point.

MEET THE **RANGER NATURALIST** AT **JENNY LAKE MUSEUM**

for **ALL DAY HIKES**
NATURE WALKS
CAMPFIRE—
PROGRAMS

A FREE GOVERNMENT SERVICE
GRAND TETON
NATIONAL **PARK**
U.S. DEPARTMENT
OF THE INTERIOR
NATIONAL PARK
SERVICE

1929

GRAND TETON N.P.

Wyoming
Est. February 26, 1929
310,634 acres (135,709 ha)

The Tetons have loomed up grandly against the sky. From this point it is perhaps the finest pictorial range in the United States or even North America.

—Thomas Moran

The Tetons, thrust upward through the earth's cracked crust millions of years ago, dominate the dramatic alpine landscape of Grand Teton National Park in northwestern Wyoming. Elevations in the park range from 6,400 feet (1,950 m) at the Snake River Plain to 13,770 feet (4,197 m) at the summit of Grand Teton. The topography is all the more dramatic by the fact that the mountains rise directly from the valley floor. The park houses 60 mammal species, some 300 species of birds, and a number of game fish, each of which has adapted to life in this rugged, often unforgiving land. Winter is brutally cold, but in summer the land glories with wildflowers in the valley and the sight and the sounds of animals free to graze and hunt in this pristine, protected environment.

Jenny Lake, formed some 12,000 years ago as a result of glacial activity, is one of the park's highlights. This location was chosen to represent Grand Teton National Park on one of the first WPA park posters ever produced. The original Grant Teton poster, printed in 1938, was the first national parks art designed by the Federal Art Project. It was printed using only four colors, with stylized fonts, and featured the Jenny Lake Museum. Three original posters survive: one is displayed at the museum, another remains in park archives, and a third is in a private collection.

NATURALIST SERVICE

SO THAT YOU MAY ENJOY THE GREAT SMOKIES ALL THE MORE

- NATURE WALKS
- ALL DAY HIKES
- LECTURES

A FREE GOVERNMENT SERVICE

GREAT SMOKY MOUNTAINS

NATIONAL

EST. 1934

PARK...

NATIONAL PARK SERVICE ....

U.S. DEPARTMENT OF THE INTERIOR

MADE BY W·P·A·-C·C·C·

GREAT SMOKY MOUNTAINS N.P.

North Carolina, Tennessee
Est. June 15, 1934
522,427 acres (211,419 ha)

I remember something that my granny told me once about these misty mountains of ours they call the Smokies. Granny said God hung that haze on purpose, to hide these hills from the folks up in Heaven who was raised here, so they wouldn't look down and be homesick.

—Vicki Lane

In addition to its unparalleled variety of plant and animal life—including 65 species of mammals, 200 varieties of birds, and 1,600 species of flowering plants—Great Smoky Mountains National Park preserves thousands of years of cultural history, from prehistoric peoples to European settlement. Within the park's 800 square miles (2,072 km^2) of mountainous terrain, 384 miles (618 km) are mountain roads that allow easy access to hiking trails, "Quiet Walkways," and historic landmarks testifying to centuries of rural mountain life and subsequent development. The Smoky Mountains, some of the oldest on earth, straddle the border between North Carolina and Tennessee, and their matchless combination of natural beauty and cultural significance draws upwards of 11 million visitors annually, making it the most visited of America's national parks.

Created from archived negatives of the original poster design, the Great Smoky Mountains poster draws attention to the lure of the region's dense forests and seasonal foliage. The view features Chimney Tops from the Newfound Gap Road, which, in addition to being the lowest point through the mountains, is the main road through the park (also known as U.S. 441), and connects Gatlinburg, Tennessee, with Cherokee, North Carolina. The colors on this poster are estimated from historic park brochures, as the original poster has never been found.

RANGER NATURALIST SERVICE

HEADQUARTERS
LOOMIS MEMORIAL
AT MANZANITA LAKE

LECTURES
HIKES
MOTOR CARAVANS
CAMPFIRE PROGRAMS
INFORMATION

SEASON
LATE JUNE TO MID SEPTEMBER

LASSEN VOLCANIC
NATIONAL PARK
U.S. DEPARTMENT
OF THE INTERIOR
NATIONAL PARK
SERVICE

EST. 1916

LASSEN VOLCANIC N.P.

California
Est. August 9, 1916
106,372 acres (43,047 ha)

The eruption came on gradually at first . . . until finally it broke out in a roar like thunder. The smoke cloud was hurled with tremendous velocity many miles high.

> —B. F. Loomis, photographer of
> 1914–15 Lassen Peak eruptions

O ver the last 300,000 years, more than 30 volcanic domes have erupted within what is now Lassen Volcanic National Park, the largest being Lassen Peak. The park is like a hydrothermal laboratory, a landscape marked by crumbled mountains and barren land disturbed by the presence of every kind of known hydrothermal feature, with the exception of geysers. The terrain bubbles, hisses, and boils with fumaroles, mud pots, and steaming ground, and the area is distinguished as one of the few locations on earth where four types of volcano exist: plug dome (Lassen Peak is the largest plug dome volcano in the world); stratovolcano; shield volcano; and cinder cone. Cataclysmic eruptions of Lassen Peak took place from 1914 to 1917. The mountain has slumbered since 1921. Rain and snowmelt in the higher elevations, where mixed conifer forest and subalpine zone supports wildlife such as bear, beaver, bobcat, and other species commonly found in the western mountains, feeds the hydrothermal system.

The re-colored poster (opposite), the next to the last of the 14 posters printed by park service WPA artists in Berkeley, California, shows erupting Lassen Peak reflected in the waters of Summit Lake. The original WPA poster, recently discovered (above), is predominantly brown, pink, green, and yellow.

RANGER NATURALIST SERVICE

LONGMIRE   PARADISE VALLEY   YAKIMA PARK   OHANAPECOSH

ILLUSTRATED EVENING
PROGRAMS

NATURE HIKES
AND FIELD TRIPS

MUSEUMS

TRAILSIDE EXHIBITS

NATURE TRAILS

PUBLICATIONS

GENERAL INFORMATION

MADE BY WPA-CCC

MOUNT RAINIER
NATIONAL PARK

1899

U.S. DEPT. OF INTERIOR • NATIONAL PARK SERVICE

MOUNT RAINIER N.P.

Washington
Est. March 2, 1899
236,381 acres (95,660 ha)

There are plenty of higher mountains, but it is the decided isolation—the absolute standing alone in full majesty of its own mightiness—that forms the attraction of Rainier.

—Paul Fountain

Standing over 14,400 feet (4,390 m) high, Mount Rainier, an active volcano and the highest peak in the Cascade Range, dominates the park's landscape from virtually every angle, but the park's grandeur only begins there. Located only 65 miles (105 km) from Seattle, Mount Rainier National Park feels like a world away. This wild wonderland boasts 25 major glaciers and over 35 miles (56 km) of permanent ice and snow cover; over 900 species of plants, including hundreds of wildflowers that explode across meadows (fittingly named Paradise) June through August; countless waterfalls and hundreds of lakes and rivers; and old-growth forests with fir trees over 1,000 years old. The 93-mile (150 km) Wonderland Trail creates a challenging backpacking loop around the entirety of Mount Rainier, an undulating trek that can be done without interruption in about 10 days, or in smaller increments from nine accessible trailheads. Known as one of the snowiest places on earth, Rainier attracts 2 million visitors annually; more than 10,000 of those attempt the climb to the summit, but only roughly half of them succeed.

Two versions of the Mount Rainier poster currently exist; the first was reproduced using a black-and-white photo as reference, and contemporary inks (above). The discovery of two original posters prompted a limited edition reprint (opposite) for the park's centennial, with the colors more faithful to the original palette.

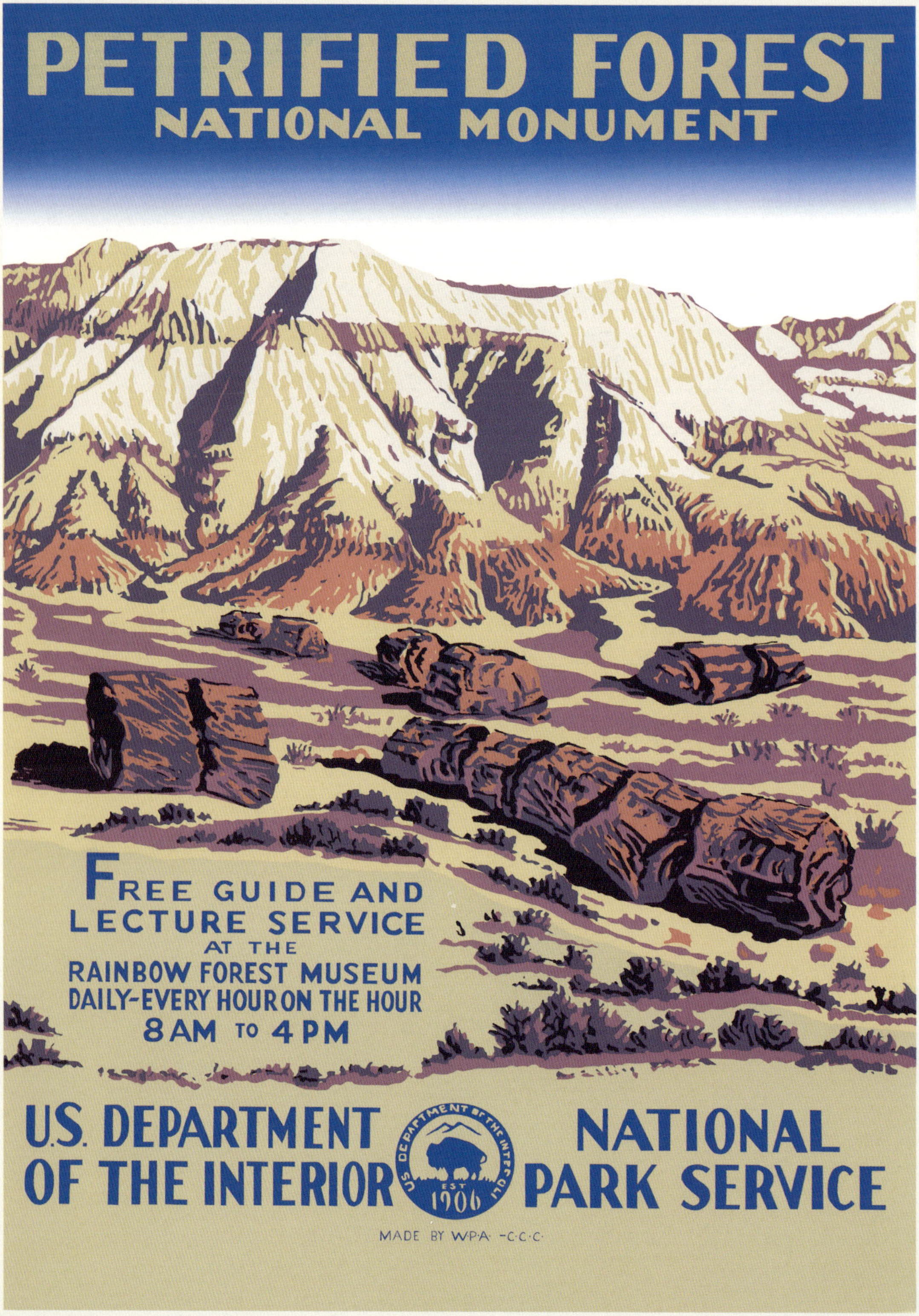
PETRIFIED FOREST
NATIONAL MONUMENT
FREE GUIDE AND
LECTURE SERVICE
AT THE
RAINBOW FOREST MUSEUM
DAILY-EVERY HOUR ON THE HOUR
8 AM TO 4 PM
U.S. DEPARTMENT
OF THE INTERIOR
NATIONAL
PARK SERVICE
MADE BY W.P.A. -C.C.C.

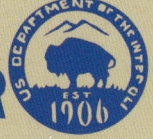

PETRIFIED FOREST N.P.

Arizona
Est. December 9, 1962; December 8, 1906 (N.M.)
221,621 acres (89,687 ha)

It is imperative to maintain portions of the wilderness untouched
so that a tree will rot where it falls . . . and moderns may at least
see what their ancestors knew in their nerves and blood.
—Bernard DeVoto

Although remnants of ancient housing and artifacts date human habitation here to about 13,000 years ago, the area that is now Petrified Forest National Park was first inhabited by dinosaurs over 200 million years ago. The landscape looked vastly different; grasslands and forests were kept green by rivers and rainfall, and nomadic peoples hunted the large game—mammoth and bison—that roamed nearby. The climate became warmer and drier but periodic flooding and volcanic eruptions uprooted trees subsequently swept away and covered by mud, ash, and an ocean that eventually dried up. When the logs were again exposed millions of years later, the petrification process had turned them into colorful gemstones that remain the park's main attraction. Blue Mesa, Jasper Forest, Crystal Forest, and Rainbow Forest are the main areas of petrification, but other park highlights include petroglyphs, archaeological ruins, spring wildflower blooms, and breathtaking vistas. Together with the adjacent Painted Desert, Petrified Forest is a haunting environment.

Reworking an earlier poster with the same historic design, the newest restoration is an authentic reproduction of original colors and screens. This poster uses a split fountain skyline, exposed petrified logs, and distant badlands to illustrate features of the park. Petrified Forest was designated as a national monument in 1906 and became a national park in 1962.

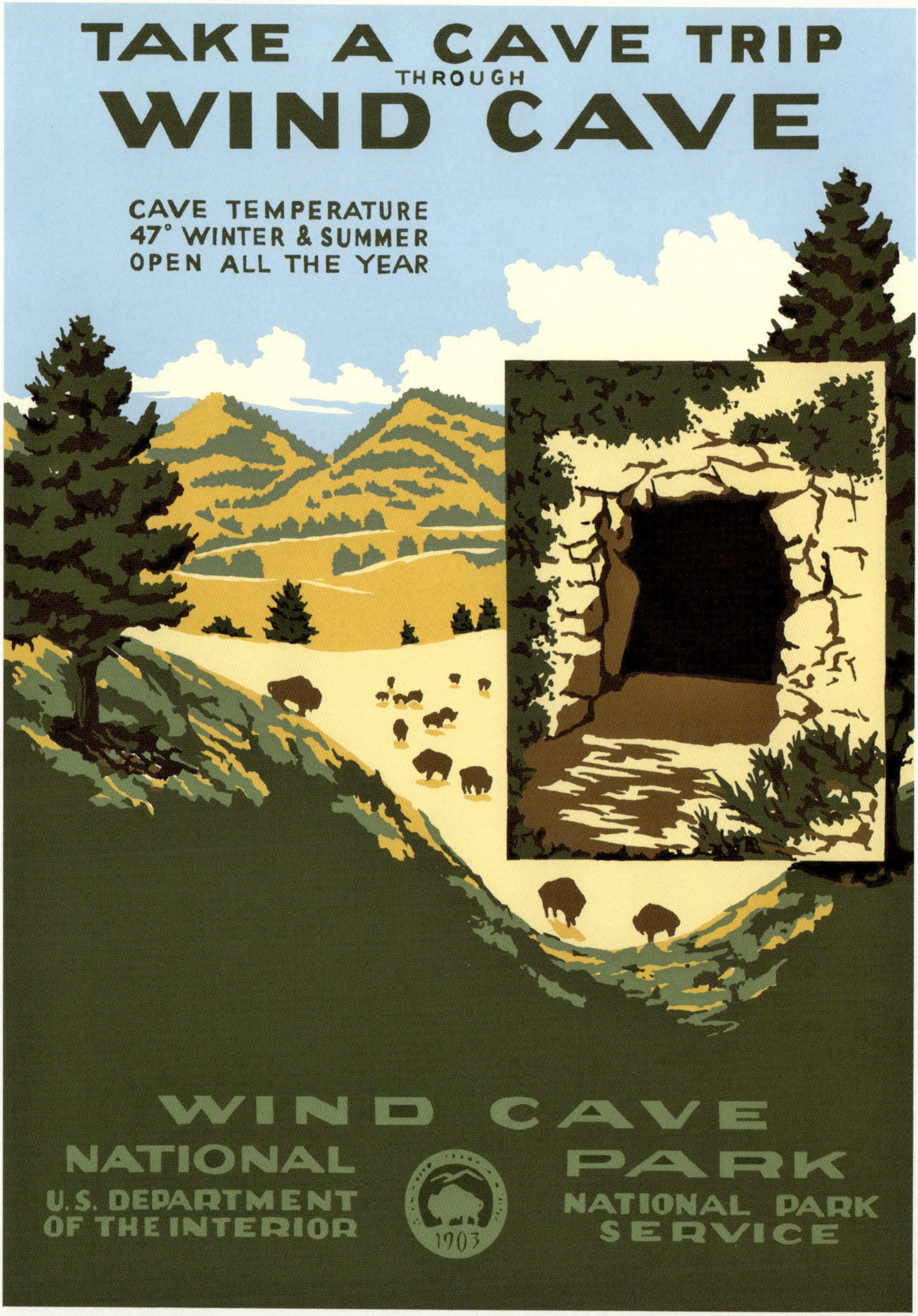

TAKE A CAVE TRIP
THROUGH
WIND CAVE

CAVE TEMPERATURE
47° WINTER & SUMMER
OPEN ALL THE YEAR

WIND CAVE
NATIONAL
PARK
U.S. DEPARTMENT
OF THE INTERIOR
NATIONAL PARK
SERVICE

1903

WIND CAVE N.P.
South Dakota
Est. January 9, 1903
28,295 acres (11,450 ha)

Wind Cave in the Black Hills was the cave from which Wakan Tanka, the Great Mystery, sent the buffalo out to the Sioux hunting grounds.

—Chief White Bull

American Indians had considered Wind Cave sacred ground for centuries before it was "discovered" in 1881 by the Bingham brothers, who followed a loud whistling noise to the cave's only natural entrance. Fascinated by the winds blowing in and out of the cave—the wind is actually caused by differences in atmospheric pressure that occur between the cave's interior and the exterior surface—explorers and entrepreneurs began staking claims in and around the cave opening, and the labyrinth below ground was developed for tourism. When a feud over rights to the cave landed in court, the Department of the Interior reclaimed the area and Wind Cave soon became the country's eighth national park. Today over 140 miles (225 km) of passages have been mapped; in addition to being one of the longest caves in the world, it is well known for its abundance of boxwork, an unusual calcite formation resembling asymmetrical honeycomb. Above ground, the surrounding prairies and forests are home to a unique ecosystem that supports bison, elk, prairie dogs, falcons, wild turkey, and more.

No original WPA posters of Wind Cave have been found. This poster features a close-up of the original cave entrance and a free-roaming bison herd in the background. It was re-created from a historic black-and-white photograph and uses modern inks to match colors used in various period park brochures.

RANGER NATURALIST SERVICE

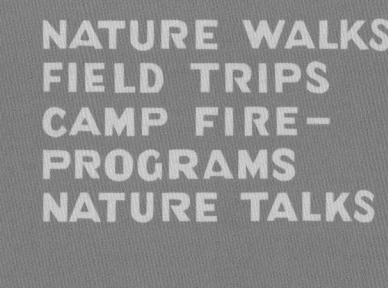

NATURE WALKS
FIELD TRIPS
CAMP FIRE-
PROGRAMS
NATURE TALKS

YELLOWSTONE
NATIONAL  PARK

U.S. DEPARTMENT
OF THE INTERIOR

NATIONAL PARK
SERVICE

YELLOWSTONE N.P.

Wyoming, Montana, Idaho
Est. March 1, 1872
2,221,766 acres (899,117 ha)

*There can be nothing in the world more beautiful than the
Yosemite, the groves of the giant sequoias and redwoods, the
Canyon of the Colorado, the Canyon of the Yellowstone,
the Three Tetons; and our people should see to it that they are
preserved for their children and their children's children forever,
with their majestic beauty all unmarred.*
                    —President Theodore Roosevelt

Yellowstone National Park, the first national park in the U.S., was established in 1872. Its early reputation was built upon the vast geothermal areas—hot springs, geysers, fumeroles—that abound within the park's boundaries. Four mountain ranges traverse the park, and more than 290 waterfalls grace the interior, the most celebrated being the Lower Falls of the Yellowstone. More than 60 mammal species, including the gray wolf, grizzly bear, bison, and elk, inhabit this remarkable reserve, and the land successfully supports close to 2,000 species of plants and thermophiles.

The serigraph pictured is faithful to the original Yellowstone National Park poster that was discovered in a second-hand store in 2004, purchased for $70, and later sold at auction for $6,000 to the Library of Congress. It is believed to have been designed by WPA artist Chester Don Powell, and was first published between September 1938 and the summer of 1939. The colors used in the 1995 WPA re-creation (see following page) were taken from brochures available at the time, as the original poster had not yet been discovered.

RANGER NATURALIST SERVICE

NATURE WALKS
FIELD TRIPS
CAMP FIRE-
PROGRAMS
NATURE TALKS

YELLOWSTONE
NATIONAL PARK
U.S. DEPARTMENT
OF THE INTERIOR
EST.
1872
NATIONAL PARK
SERVICE

ABOVE: Yellowstone N.P.—Old Faithful
This 1995 re-creation of the Yellowstone National Park poster—Old Faithful's steam billowing against a blue sky streaked with orange plumes—was created before the 2004 discovery of the original Old Faithful poster.

BELOW AND OPPOSITE: Yellowstone N.P.—Lower Yellowstone Falls
The deep, intense colors used in this contemporary poster of Yellowstone's Lower Falls (BELOW) were based on information in brochures of the WPA era, as no such WPA poster was known to exist when the print was re-created in 1995. This coloration has since been discontinued. The Lower Yellowstone Falls poster (OPPOSITE) was re-created using the six colors found on the original poster, which was discovered in 2004.

RANGER NATURALIST SERVICE
HEADQUARTERS YELLOWSTONE MUSEUMS

NATURE WALKS
FIELD TRIPS
CAMP FIRE PROGRAMS
ILLUSTRATED TALKS
AND MUSEUM SERVICE

YELLOWSTONE
NATIONAL PARK
U.S. DEPARTMENT
OF THE INTERIOR
EST.
1872
NATIONAL PARK
SERVICE

RANGER NATURALIST SERVICE

HEADQUARTERS YOSEMITE MUSEUM

AUTO CARAVANS
NATURE WALKS
MUSEUM LECTURES
ILLUSTRATED TALKS
ALL-DAY HIKES
CAMP-FIRE PROGRAMS
SEVEN-DAY HIKES
JUNIOR NATURE SCHOOL
WILDFLOWER GARDEN
INDIAN DEMONSTRATIONS
NATURALIST STATIONED AT
MARIPOSA GROVE MUSEUM,
GLACIER POINT, AND
TUOLUMNE MEADOWS

YOSEMITE
NATIONAL PARK

U.S. DEPARTMENT
OF THE INTERIOR

NATIONAL PARK
SERVICE

YOSEMITE N.P.

California
Est. October 1, 1890
748,036 acres (302,719 ha)

Yosemite Valley, to me, is always a sunrise, a glitter of green and golden wonder in a vast edifice of stone and space.

—Ansel Adams

An estimated 3.3 million visitors come to Yosemite National Park every year, around 90 percent of them to Yosemite Valley, whose stunning scenery is marked by monumental domes and pinnacles that pierce the broad expanse of sky, as well as stunningly beautiful waterfalls. Upon entering the valley, a short but steep trail leads to 620-foot (189 m) Bridalveil Fall, which thunders during spring and showers with mist the rest of the year. Opposite Bridalveil Fall rises El Capitan, the largest granite monolith in the world. The valley also boasts splendid Yosemite Falls, at 2,425 feet (739 m) the tallest waterfall in North America. But the valley comprises only about one percent of Yosemite's total area, the remainder of the park offering hundreds of miles of hiking trails and roads that promise a High Sierra wilderness experience that encompasses the valley and the near desert, the heights, the mid-elevation forest, and the mountains. The importance of protecting these natural treasures prompted President Abraham Lincoln to sign a congressional bill in 1864 stating that Yosemite Valley and the Mariposa Grove be granted to the state of California as an inalienable public trust. Thus, for the first time in history, a country formally set land aside as a wilderness preserve.

The iconic face of El Capitan, in the heart of Yosemite Valley, is featured on the WPA poster pictured. This poster belongs to the original WPA poster series. It was re-created here from archived negatives, and its colors are true to those used in the original poster.

ZION N.P.

Utah

Est. November 19, 1919

148,733 acres (60,190 ha)

There is an eloquence to their forms which stirs the imagination with a singular power and kindles in the mind . . . a glowing response . . . Nothing can exceed the wondrous beauty of Zion . . . in the nobility and beauty of the sculptures there is no comparison.

—Clarence E. Dutton

Mormon settlers, awed by the dramatic landscape of soaring Navajo sandstone cliffs smoldering in shades of cream, pink, and red where the Virgin River and its tributaries sculpt the land, called the canyon Little Zion for its resemblance to the biblical heavenly city of God. Exposed layered rock reveals 240 million years of earth's history. With a difference in elevation of roughly 5,000 feet (1,524 m) between the park's lowest point, at Coal Pits Wash, to its highest, at Horse Ranch Mountain, the area supports a wide variety of flora and fauna. The high plateaus where fir and pine flourish surrender to cottonwood, willow, and box elder that line the streams, and cactus and juniper on the desert floor. Reptiles, mammals, birds, and amphibians find sanctuary amid the abundant plant life.

This poster (opposite), showing a view of Great White Throne, is an original WPA design. It was re-created from black-and-white films, with its colors interpreted from materials of the time period. The colors were chosen to represent the site at sunset; however, the colors on the original Zion poster (see the original on this page, top right) are notably brighter and lighter, with shades of blue, magenta, cream, and green.

SEE AMERICA
UNITED STATES TRAVEL BUREAU
MADE BY WORKS PROGRESS ADMINISTRATION · FEDERAL ART PROJECT NYC

SEE AMERICA

Arches N.P., Est. April 12, 1929 (N.M.)

Carlsbad Caverns N.P.,
   Est. May 14, 1930

Glacier N.P., Est. May 11, 1910

The "See America" poster prints were not included in the National Park Service poster set published in Berkeley. They were produced by the New York poster project for the United States Travel Bureau, which later became part of the U.S. Department of the Interior, and whose banner appears on each poster. Designed with bold, handsome imagery accompanied by a short, but explicit message, the "See America" prints were created to encourage tourism. Opposite, the poster features Double Arch in Arches National Park; at top right, the scene is the Big Room in Carlsbad Caverns National Park; and at bottom right, the dramatic terrain of Glacier National Park—what John Muir called "the best care-killing scenery on the continent"—is pictured. The Glacier National Park poster is a contemporary poster created from an original half-finished sketch from the "See America" series by the New York poster project.

102 FEET
CIRCUMFERENCE
AT BASE

CONTEMPORARY WPA NATIONAL PARK POSTERS

National parks are the best idea we ever had.
Absolutely American, absolutely democratic,
they reflect us at our best rather than our worst.
— Wallace Stegner

ACADIA N.P.

Maine
Est. February 26, 1919
49,600 acres (20,000 ha)

To stand at the edge of the sea, to sense the ebb and flow of the tides, to feel the breath of a mist moving over a great salt marsh, to watch the flight of shore birds that have swept up and down the surf lines of the continents for untold thousands of years . . . is to have knowledge of things that are as nearly eternal as any earthly life can be.

—Rachel Carson

The majority of Acadia National Park is on Mount Desert Island, named L'Isle des Monts Déserts (island of barren mountains) by Samuel de Champlain, who explored the region in 1604. By the mid-19th century, the considerable charms of coastal Maine had attracted "summer people," many of them wealthy, whose desire to preserve the natural beauty of the place resulted in donated land that became the core of the park. Originally Lafayette National Park, its name was changed in 1929 to Acadia National Park. The park's area increased piecemeal, its current boundaries not officially determined by Congress until 1986. Among the highlights of Acadia National Park is Cadillac Mountain, whose summit, from October 7 to March 6, is the first location in the U.S. from which to see the sunrise.

Bass Harbor Lighthouse, established in 1858 on the southwest side of Mount Desert Island, was chosen for inclusion on the poster shown, which is a new poster design that follows the original WPA style. The Acadia serigraph is one of seven posters that were printed using a split fountain technique, where multiple colors are simultaneously flowed together, seen here in the rendering of the water and sky.

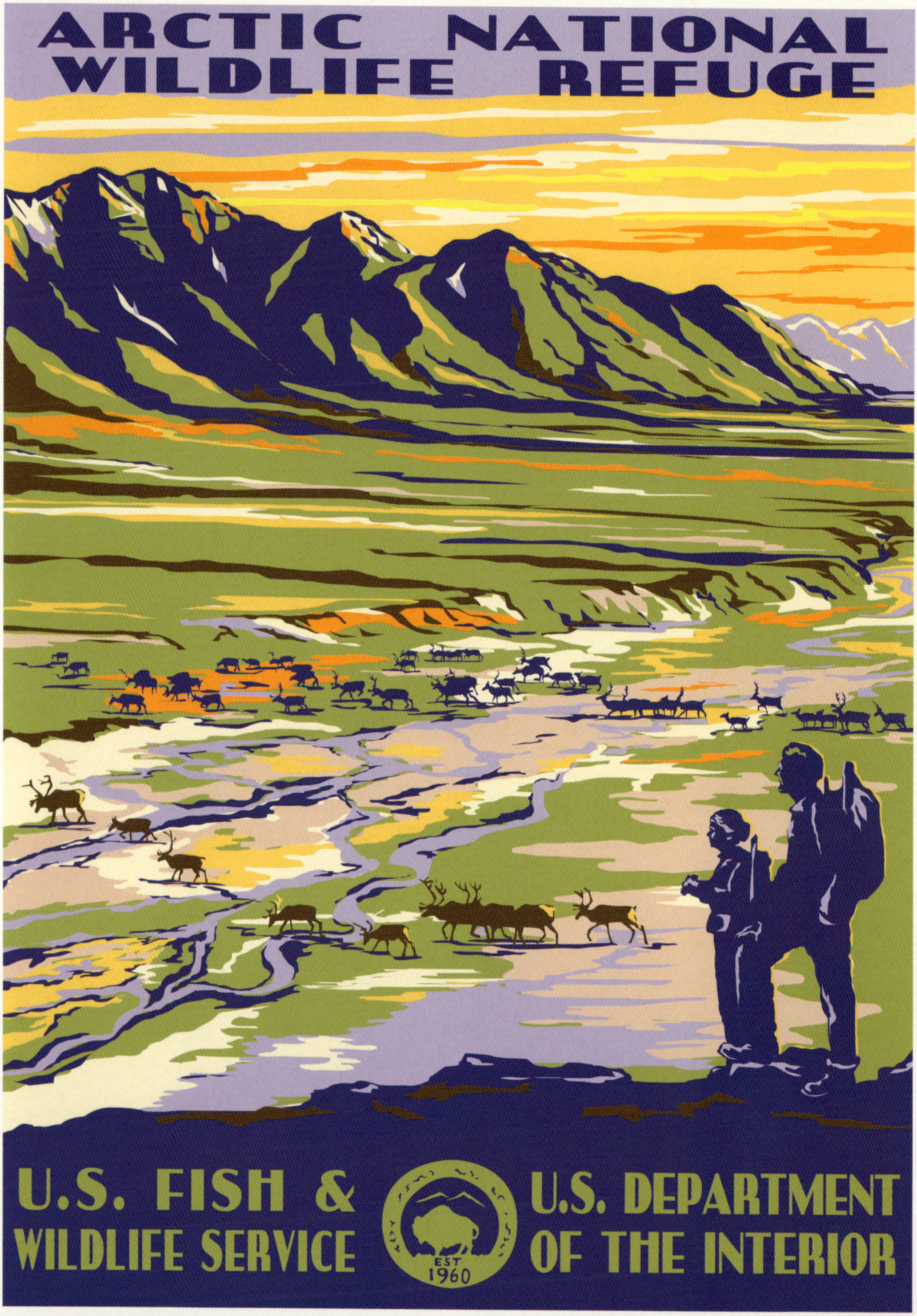
ARCTIC NATIONAL
WILDLIFE REFUGE
U.S. FISH &
WILDLIFE SERVICE
EST
1960
U.S. DEPARTMENT
OF THE INTERIOR

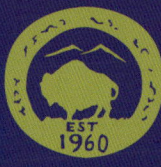

ARCTIC N.W.R.

Alaska
Est. 1960
19.6 million acres (7,931,838 ha)

Here still survives one of Planet Earth's own works of art. This one symbolizes freedom: freedom to continue, unhindered and forever if we are willing, the particular story of Planet Earth unfolding here.
—Lowell Sumner, NPS scientist

When in 1960 President Eisenhower created the Arctic National Wildlife Refuge (ANWR) "for the purpose of preserving unique wildlife, wilderness, and recreational values" it included 8.9 million acres (3,601,702 ha) of pristine wilderness in Alaska's northeast corner. In 1980, the refuge was expanded to its current 19.6 million acres (7,931,838 ha), making it one of the world's largest intact ecosystems. With nary a road nor hiking trail in sight, visitors to the refuge are truly on their own. This remarkable subarctic and arctic environmental jewel includes tundra-covered coastal plains, the remote Brooks mountain range, glaciers, and 160-plus waterways, all of which support hundreds of species of wildlife and indigenous communities that have called this place home for thousands of years. In addition to the dangers of climate change, the refuge has been repeatedly threatened by oil companies seeking to open it up to oil drilling; the 2015 Udall-Eisenhower Arctic Wilderness Act proposes to permanently protect the refuge and its coastal plain, considered the refuge's "biological heart," from drilling.

This contemporary poster design in the WPA style was created to celebrate the 50th anniversary of the ANWR. The artwork highlights the refuge's notable features, including the Brooks Range, the Sheenjek River, the migrating caribou herd, and silhouettes of Olaus and Mardy Murie, passionate protectors of the Alaskan wilderness.

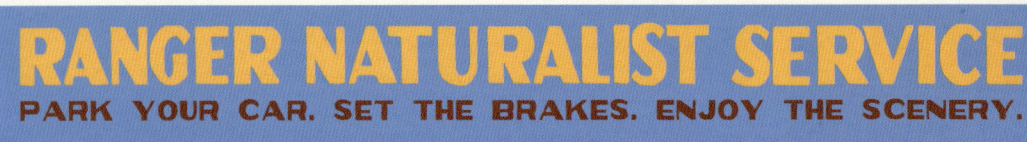

RANGER NATURALIST SERVICE

PARK YOUR CAR. SET THE BRAKES. ENJOY THE SCENERY.

DISCOVER 30 MILLION YEAR OLD FOSSILS:
TITANOTHERE "THE HUGE THUNDERBEAST"
HYAENODON "THE FLESH-EATING CARNIVORE"
ARCHAEOTHERIUM "THE GIANT SWINE"
MESOHIPPUS "THE THREE-TOED HORSE"

BADLANDS

NATIONAL

MONUMENT

U.S. DEPARTMENT
OF THE INTERIOR

NATIONAL PARK
SERVICE

EST. 1939

BADLANDS N.P.

South Dakota

Est. November 10, 1978; January 29, 1939 (N.M.)

244,300 acres (98,865 ha)

The wilderness holds answers to questions man has not yet learned to ask.

—Nancy Newhall

The supernatural landscape of the Dakota Badlands has a haunting allure. Created by millions of years of water and wind erosion, the ragged pinnacles of The Wall stand watch over a seemingly desolate but surprisingly life-filled landscape. Known by the Lakota as *mako sica* or "land bad," the region was also known to early French trappers who described it as "bad lands to travel across." Badlands National Park's distinctive geologic shapes began to emerge roughly 70 million years ago during the Cretaceous Period with deposits of shale, which are visible as a black layer at the base of many of the region's stone formations. Erosion continues to sculpt and shape the land. In addition to its remarkable stone topography, which contains some of the world's richest fossil beds, Badlands National Park is home to mixed-grass prairies which support numerous species of reptiles, birds, and small and large mammals, including bison, which sustained the early nomadic tribes and Oglala Lakota nation, for whom these lands are sacred.

The multi-hued rendition of the Badlands poster, a new design in the style of the original artworks, draws attention to the layers of deposits that make up the harsh but mesmerizing rock monuments in the park. The color bands indicate the layers' different origins and dates. Poster copy promises a close-encounter experience with plenty of fossilized evidence of the area's oldest residents.

RANGER NATURALIST SERVICE

EXPLORE THE BASIN IN THE HEART OF THE CHISOS MOUNTAINS

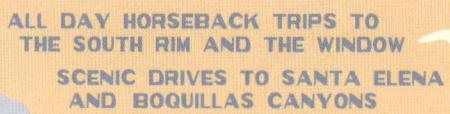

ALL DAY HORSEBACK TRIPS TO
THE SOUTH RIM AND THE WINDOW

SCENIC DRIVES TO SANTA ELENA
AND BOQUILLAS CANYONS

STAY
AT THE
HACIENDA
COTTAGES
BELOW
CASA GRANDE

BUILT BY THE CCC

BIG BEND
NATIONAL PARK

U.S. DEPARTMENT
OF THE INTERIOR

NATIONAL PARK
SERVICE

U.S. DEPARTMENT OF THE INTERIOR

EST 1944

BIG BEND N.P.

Texas
Est. June 12, 1944
801,163 acres (324,219 ha)

There is much the government can do and should do to improve the environment. But even more important is the individual who plants a tree or cleans a corner of neglect. For it is the individual who himself benefits, and also protects a heritage of beauty for his children and future generations.

—Lady Bird Johnson

Big Bend National Park is a vast wilderness cradled in a "big bend" in the Rio Grande river as it makes its way from El Paso to the Gulf of Mexico. Big Bend is primarily Chihuahuan desert, a starkly beautiful terrain that can explode with colorful wildflowers after a soaking rain. The Chisos Mountains, which rise in the center of the park, provide cool respite from the lowlands. Grasslands dotted with shrubs comprise the divide between mountain and desert, adding further to the ecological diversity within the park.

Big Bend houses some 1,200 species of plants, from desert willow, skeleton-leaf goldeneye, and blackfoot daisy in the desert to sotol, Torrey yucca, and cholla in the grasslands, and pine, oak, and juniper on the high slopes. At least 450 different bird species populate Big Bend—more than in any other national park—the most sought by birders being the Colima warbler. Mountain wildlife including black bears, mountain lions, and deer roam the higher elevations.

The region has a rich cultural history—American Indians, Spanish explorers, the U.S. military, and a fair number of outlaws among the mix. The popular Roosevelt Stone Cottages featured in this contemporary poster were built by the Civilian Conservation Corps and are still used for lodging by park visitors today.

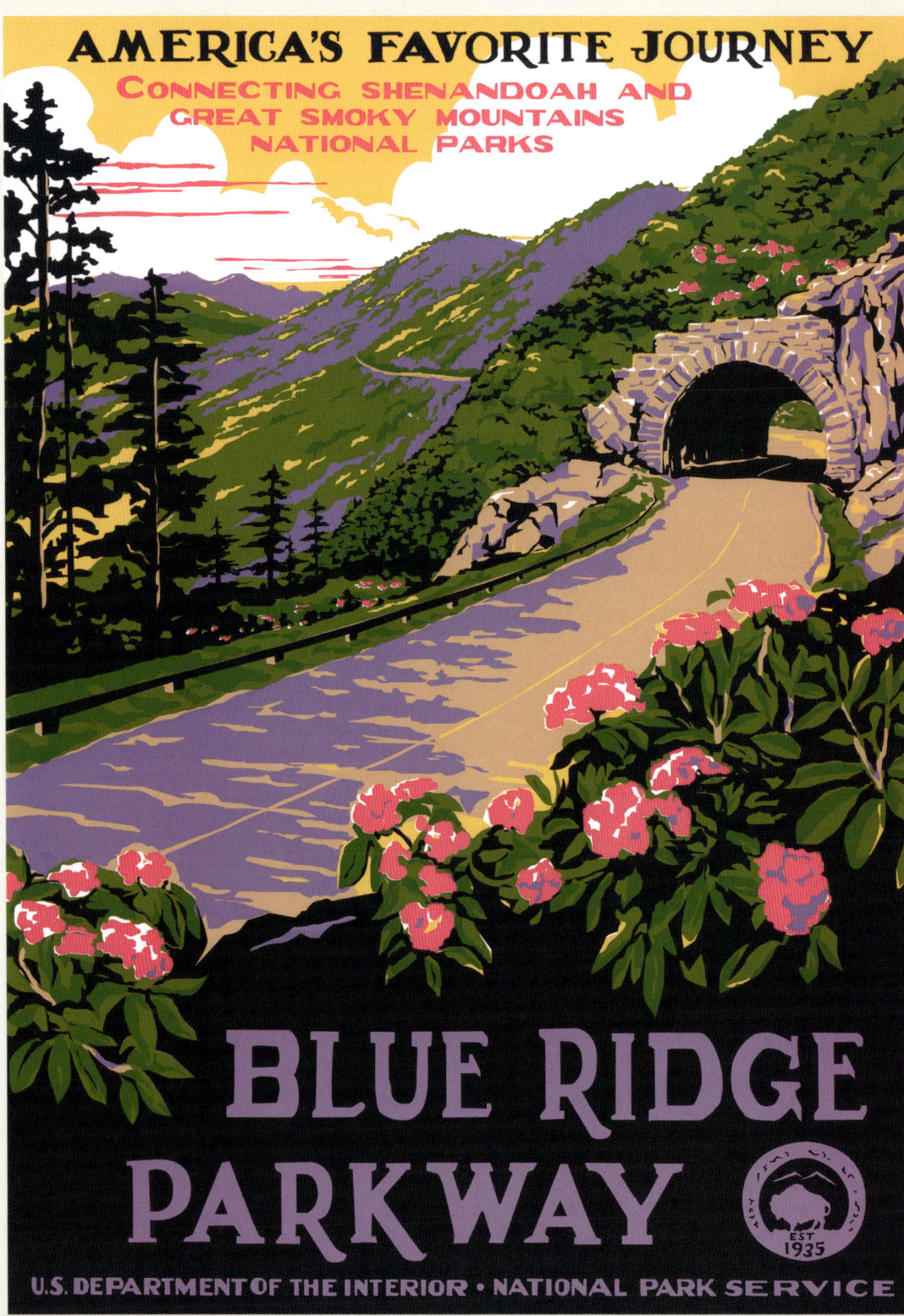

BLUE RIDGE PARKWAY

North Carolina, Virginia
Est. June 30, 1936
469 miles (755 km)

Thousands of tired, nerve-shaken, over-civilized people are beginning to find out that going to the mountains is going home; that wildness is a necessity.

—John Muir

Winding through the Appalachian Highlands along the crest of the Blue Ridge Mountains, the Blue Ridge Parkway connects Virginia's Shenandoah National Park with Great Smoky Mountains National Park in North Carolina. The parkway was begun in 1935 as part of FDR's New Deal initiative, putting to work laborers and professionals left unemployed by the Great Depression. Construction was slow, as great care was taken to keep the region's natural beauty and resources intact; the final section of road was not opened until 1987, fifty-two years after the initial groundbreaking. In addition to supporting an impressive array of plant and animal life, this bucolic mountainous landscape preserves the physical remnants of early settlement in this region, from American Indians through early pioneers, with interpretive landmarks reminding visitors of the strength and resourcefulness of the region's early cultures.

The Blue Ridge poster, a new design created in the WPA style, highlights features of this scenic road: the blue haze that gives the area its name, panoramic vistas, an explosion of roadside wildflowers, and one of the 26 tunnels on the parkway. The National Park Service constructed stone tunnels in the rustic style to blend in with the natural environment, much of the stone taken from quarries near the site.

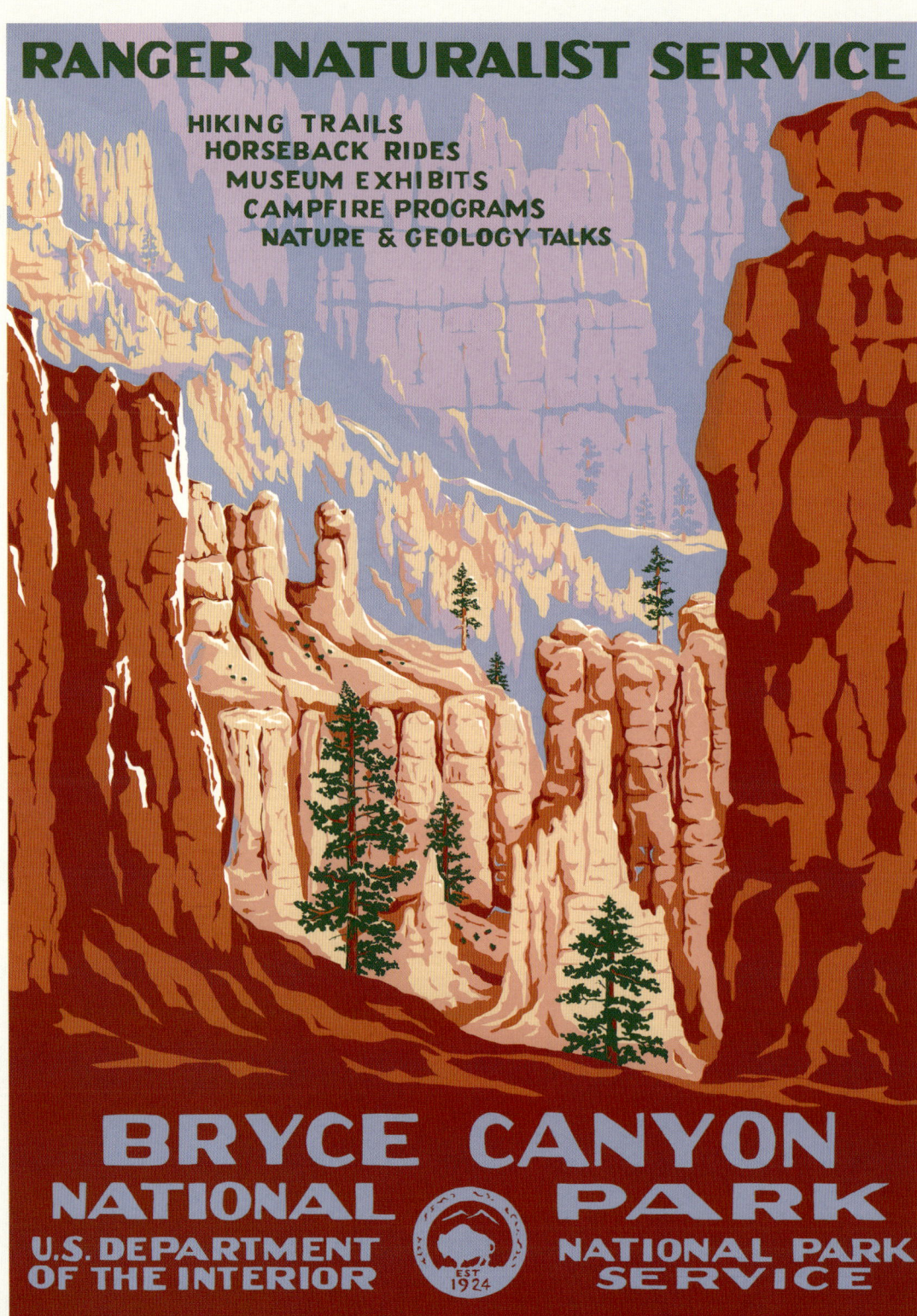

BRYCE CANYON N.P.
Utah
Est. February 28, 1928; June 8, 1923 (N.M.)
35,835 acres (14,500 ha)

The national park idea has been nurtured by each succeeding generation of Americans. Today, across our land, the National Park System represents America at its best.
— George B. Hartzog Jr., NPS Director, 1964–72

Small in size compared to several of the other national parks that grace the American Southwest, Bryce Canyon National Park nevertheless boasts some of the most spectacular natural topography in the national park system. Named for Mormon pioneer Ebenezer Bryce, Bryce Canyon is made up of legions of varied limestone formations—slot canyons, windows, fins, and spires dubbed "hoodoos" for their peculiar resemblance to strange human forms—which are located along the edge of the Paunsaugunt Plateau, part of the Grand Staircase layers of rock that also includes the Grand Canyon.

Bordering the rim of the plateau, ponderosa pines stand sentinel, meadows carpet high elevations, and forests are dense with fir-spruce, all comprising environments that welcome and sustain a wide variety of wildlife. The panoramic view from this prospect includes three states, and some of the cleanest air on earth enables close to 200 miles (322 km) of visibility.

The Bryce Canyon poster was the first poster designed on a computer. The colors derive from photographs taken during the fire season, explaining the bluish tint that represents the atmospheric conditions, and also serve artistically to heighten the contrast in the composition. This and the Shenandoah poster are the only contemporary posters created without the inclusion of sky.

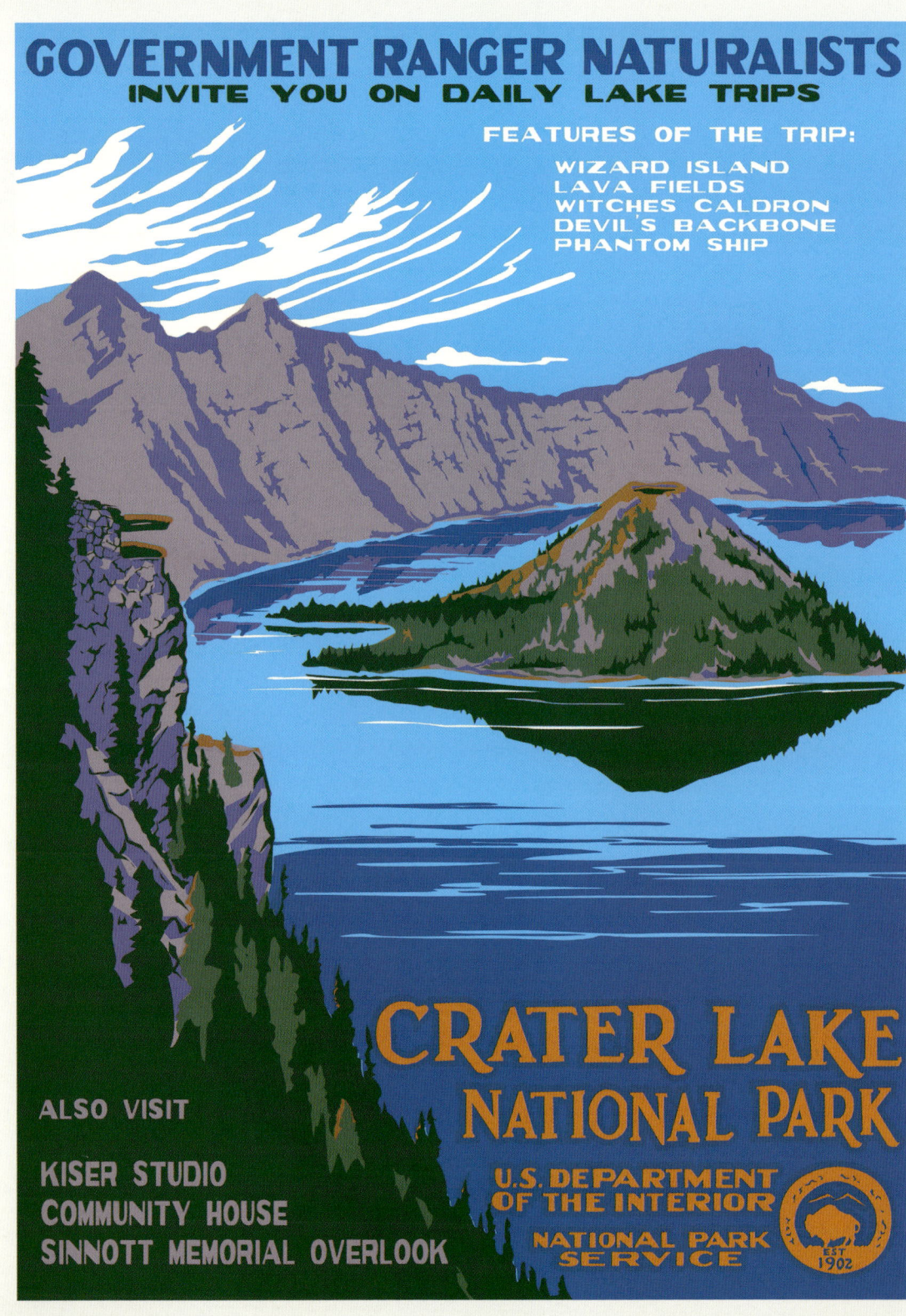

GOVERNMENT RANGER NATURALISTS
INVITE YOU ON DAILY LAKE TRIPS

FEATURES OF THE TRIP:
WIZARD ISLAND
LAVA FIELDS
WITCHES CALDRON
DEVIL'S BACKBONE
PHANTOM SHIP

CRATER LAKE
NATIONAL PARK

U.S. DEPARTMENT
OF THE INTERIOR

NATIONAL PARK
SERVICE

EST 1902

ALSO VISIT

KISER STUDIO
COMMUNITY HOUSE
SINNOTT MEMORIAL OVERLOOK

CRATER LAKE N.P.
Oregon
Est. May 22, 1902
183,224 acres (74,188 ha)

My heart bounds with joy and gladness, for I realize that I have been the cause of opening up this wonderful lake for the pleasure of mankind, millions of whom will come and enjoy and unborn generations will profit by its glories.
   —William Gladstone Steel, Supt. of Crater Lake Park, 1913–16

Willliam Gladstone Steel's visit to Crater Lake in 1885 fulfilled a childhood promise he had made to himself to some day see this storied "sunken lake." The site did not disappoint, and in 1902, largely owing to his tireless efforts, Crater Lake National Park was established.

The eruption that ultimately created Crater Lake occurred roughly 7,700 years ago, and lasted only two days, during which the top of what is now called Mount Mazama blew, leaving behind an enormous crater measuring 3,900 feet (1,188 m) deep, and a caldera 5–6 miles (8–10 km) in diameter. Rain and snowmelt ultimately filled the caldera, forming what is now known as the deepest lake in the U.S., and the seventh deepest in the world. Crater Lake is also one of the world's clearest lakes, its strikingly blue water reaching a depth of more than 1,900 feet (580 m). Once all the volcanic activity subsided, hemlock, pine, fur, and wildflowers began to return, as did wildlife such as bobcats, black bears, deer, marmots, eagles, and hawks.

Created in the WPA style, the Crater Lake poster advertises some of the park's most notable and bewitching features: Wizard Island, Witches Cauldron, Devil's Backbone, among them. The Sinnott Memorial Building, dedicated in 1931, is seen jutting out from Victor Rock at left.

DEATH VALLEY N.P.

California, Nevada
Est. October 31, 1994; 1933 (N.M.)
3,372,402 acres (1,364,763 ha)

Would You Enjoy a Trip to Hell? . . . You Might Enjoy a Trip to Death Valley, Now! It has all the advantages of hell without the inconveniences.

> —April Fool's Day 1907 advertisement in the
> mining camp newspaper *Death Valley Chuck-Walla*

A mere 20 years after this good-natured quip appeared in print, a luxury hotel was built in Death Valley, proving that this swath of forbidding desert land—home to the hottest, driest, lowest place in North America—has an irresistible appeal to many. Establishing a national park here seemed appropriate to National Park Service director Stephen Mather, but due to a possible conflict of interest—the idea was initiated by the Pacific Coast Borax Company, of 20-mule-team fame, where Mather had been previously employed—Death Valley National Park was not designated until after his death.

Nearly a million visitors come to Death Valley National Park each year, drawn to brave the extreme conditions of the stark, scorching valley and to appreciate the contrast with the jagged canyons and soaring mountains where merciful cool descends. Then too, they come to bear witness to a story of survival, that of stalwart souls—American Indians and frontiersmen who lived here—and of a group of hopeful Forty-niners who faced unimaginable human suffering, giving rise to the valley's grim moniker.

The Death Valley poster harkens to the Roaring Twenties in its depiction of Death Valley Ranch, or Scotty's Castle, a fabulous home with a colorful past, touted, as seen on the poster, as "An Oasis in Grapevine Canyon."

DENALI N.P. AND PRESERVE

Alaska

Est. February 26, 1917 (Mt. McKinley N.P.)

6,075,029 acres (2,458,477 ha)

Coppers and purples, and reds and golds, browns and blacks streaked across the earth violently, and sweeping up and over, a kaleidoscope of dirt and rock that challenges even the most jaded of hearts to not fall under her spell.

—Danielle Rohr, *Denali Skies*

Comprising over 6 million acres of the Alaskan wilderness—glacially-fed braided rivers, expanses of open tundra, boreal forest, soaring mountain ranges—Denali is the northern crown jewel of the National Park System. The 92-mile (148 km) Denali Park Road is the only vehicular access into the park's interior, from which the park's 500,000 annual visitors can experience an amazing variety of wildlife, unparalleled and untouched landscapes, and a glimpse of Denali, or "The High One" to native Athabaskan Indians. At 20,310 feet (6,190 m), Denali is North America's highest peak and one of the Seven Summits for experienced mountaineers. In the early 1900s, hunter-naturalist Charles Sheldon, a native Vermonter, spent the better part of a decade lobbying for Denali's national park status, having spent an entire year living in the Alaskan wilderness and convinced of the importance of protecting this last frontier and the creatures that call it home.

This new addition to the contemporary poster collection was designed in the WPA style and features the original name of the park, which shared its identity with the official moniker of the mountain until the stately peak's name was formally changed to Denali in 2015.

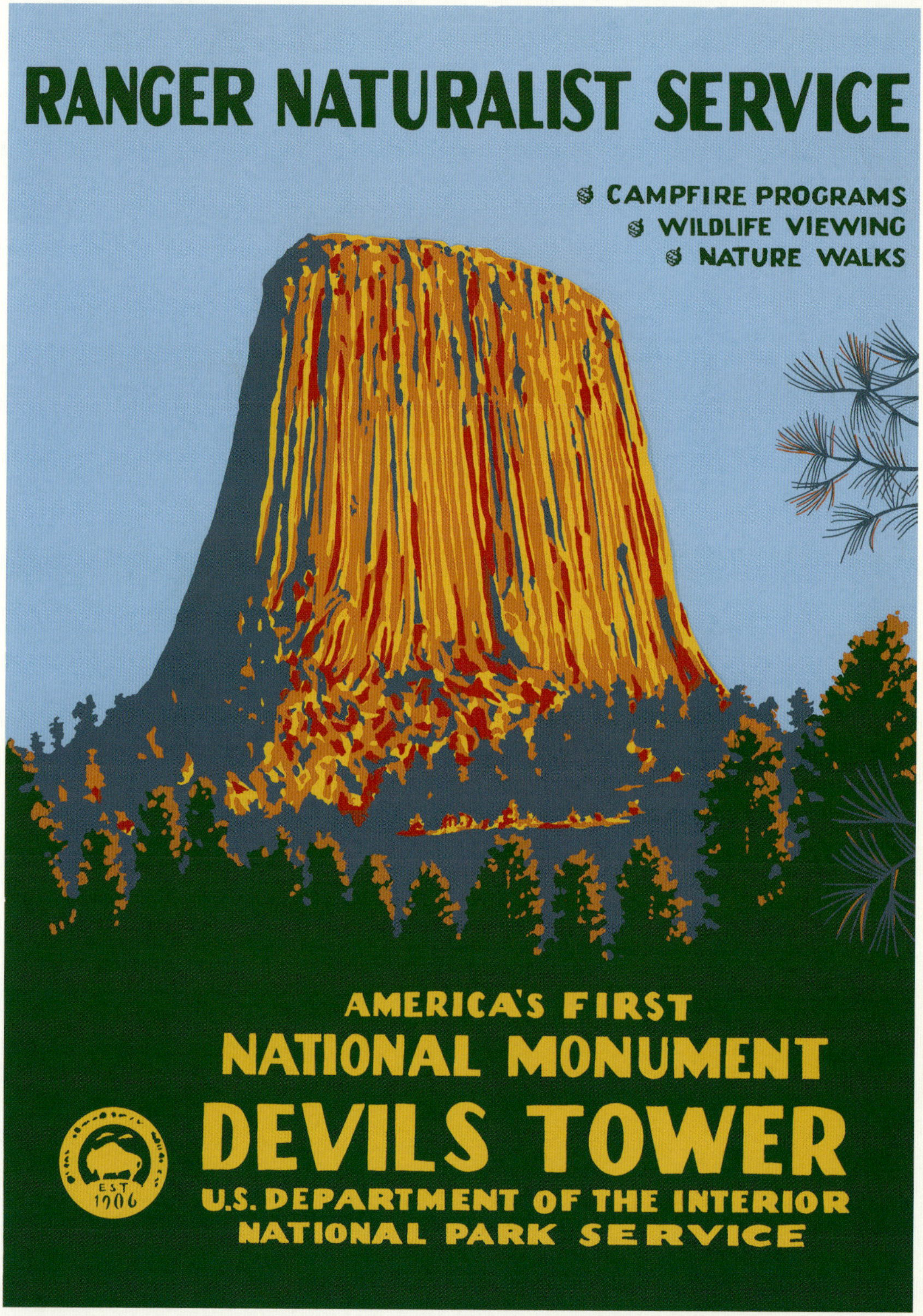

RANGER NATURALIST SERVICE

- CAMPFIRE PROGRAMS
- WILDLIFE VIEWING
- NATURE WALKS

AMERICA'S FIRST
NATIONAL MONUMENT
DEVILS TOWER
U.S. DEPARTMENT OF THE INTERIOR
NATIONAL PARK SERVICE

EST. 1906

DEVILS TOWER N.M.

Wyoming
Est. September 24, 1906
1,347 acres (545 ha)

At the top of the ridge I caught sight of Devil's Tower upthrust against the gray sky as if in the birth of time the core of the earth had broken through its crust and the motion of the world was begun.

—N. Scott Momaday

The soaring monolith that protrudes from the surrounding prairies and pine forests of Wyoming's Black Hills was the nation's first national monument, designated by President Theodore Roosevelt in 1906. Rising over 1,200 feet (3,660 m) above the Bell Fourche River, Devils Tower National Monument includes the obvious centerpiece and 1,347 acres (545 ha) of additional parkland. Formed millions of years ago by an intrusion of igneous material, erosion continually wore down the softer sedimentary covering to reveal the unique formation that exists today. The area that makes up the monument, and the tower itself, has been revered for centuries by Plains Indian tribes as a sacred site and cultural landmark. Ignoring the U.S. government's treaties with the Indians, pioneers entered and occupied these hallowed lands, renaming the tower and ascribing to it new uses.

The first contemporary poster produced in the style of the WPA, this Devils Tower artwork pays tribute to the surrounding ponderosa pine forests, and emphasizes the monolith's unique striations while creating an accurate perspective of height and form. Produced before the computer era, the artwork was first created as a painting by Doug Leen and Michael Dupille which hangs in the park superintendent's office. Subsequent editions of the Devils Tower poster featured several small changes, making the first edition unique.

DINOSAUR N.M.

Colorado, Utah
Est. October 4, 1915
210,560 acres (85,210 ha)

At last, in the top of the ledge where the softer overlying beds form a divide, a kind of saddle, I saw eight of the tail bones of [an Apatosaurus] in exact position. It was a beautiful sight.

—Earl Douglass

Paleontologist Earl Douglass's 1909 discovery of eight *Apatosaurus* bones in eastern Utah led to the unearthing of one of the world's most significant stores of dinosaur fossils—and, by 1915, the establishment of Dinosaur National Monument. In 1938, the original 80 acres (32 ha) surrounding the fossil beds was expanded to include parts of the Yampa and Green Rivers.

Though named for its former Jurassic residents, Dinosaur National Monument is far more than its famous quarry. More than 1,000 native species of plants and animals are found within its expanse. River canyons, basins, and mountains range in elevation from under 4,750 feet (1,448 m) near the quarry to over 9,000 feet (2,743 m) at Zenobia Peak. Fossils confirm that Paleo-Indians dwelled here some 7,000 years ago, and petroglyphs indicate the presence of Fremont Indians approximately 1,000 years ago. Ute and Shoshone still inhabit areas near this scientifically and culturally important land today.

The bold, contemporary design of this poster was created to highlight the iconic geologic features of Steamboat Rock at the convergence of the Green and Yampa Rivers. The text on the face of Steamboat Rock references a period around 1936 when WPA workers set up fossil exhibits and removed excavated bedrock to reveal the "Wall of Bones." And in the design, the artist has playfully concealed the silhouette of a dinosaur.

EVERGLADES N.P.

Florida
Est. December 6, 1947
1,542,526 acres (624,238 ha)

Here are no lofty peaks seeking the sky, no mighty glaciers or rushing streams wearing away the uplifted land. Here is land, tranquil in its quiet beauty, serving not as the source of water, but as the last receiver of it. To its natural abundance we owe the spectacular plant and animal life that distinguishes this place from all others in our country.
— President Harry S. Truman

During the rainy season, Everglades National Park is covered with a sheet of water about a foot deep (0.3 m), but a network of boardwalk trails allows visitors to experience the distinctiveness of this subtropical environment. This unique habitat, famous for its sawgrass prairies, mangrove forests, numerous bird species, and endangered animals including the manatee, the American crocodile, and the Florida panther, is also internationally recognized as an ecological gem; UNESCO has designated the area as a World Heritage Site as well as an International Biosphere Reserve. Development of southern Florida has diverted water from the Everglades, putting the entire ecosystem at risk. Although the Everglades' vast acreage makes it the third largest national park in the 48 contiguous states, only 25 percent of the original Everglades land remains.

This WPA-styled new poster design highlights the aquatic wildlife that make the Everglades home, especially during the rainy season. The poster features the mangrove tree, alligators, great egret, tricolored heron, and great blue heron.

GLACIER BAY N.P. AND PRESERVE

Alaska
Est. December 2, 1980; 1925 (N.M.)
3,283,246 acres (1,328,683 ha)

To the lover of pure wildness Alaska is one of the most wonderful countries in the world . . . It seems as if surely we must at length reach the very paradise of the poets, the abode of the blessed.

—John Muir

When John Muir entered southeast Alaska's Glacier Bay region in 1879, he found a glacial retreat rapidly exposing land that had been covered by ice since the last ice age. Amazingly, nature was recovering and life was returning to the land and sea. Signs of glacial activity are still everywhere, but the boundaries of Glacier Bay National Park and Preserve reveal stages of rebirth. At the southern end, forests support large mammals including bears, moose, wolves, and coyotes; further north, where the ice recession happened more recently, slopes are rugged with sparse vegetation. A rich and healthy marine environment also characterizes Glacier Bay and helps to maintain a thriving and diverse ecosystem. Tour boats through Glacier Bay's numerous inlets allow visitors to see land and marine mammals in their natural habitats; experience calving icebergs; and admire the unique landscape of mountains, valleys, fjords, tidewater glaciers, coves, and coastline. Originally Glacier Bay National Monument, the area was expanded and elevated to national park and preserve status in 1980. The park is also a UNESCO World Heritage Site and a jewel in the crown of Alaska's Inside Passage.

The Glacier Bay poster, a new design styled after the WPA series, succeeds in revealing the magnitude of the mountains and tidewater glacier by including the steamship for perspective.

GREAT SMOKY MOUNTAINS N.P.

North Carolina, Tennessee
Est. June 15, 1934
522,427 acres (211,419 ha)

Here in the Great Smokies, we have come together to dedicate these mountains, streams, and forests, to the service of the millions of American people.

—President Franklin D. Roosevelt

Great Smoky Mountains National Park was established just in time to put the Civilian Conservation Corps into action. Organized in 1933 to create jobs during the Great Depression, the CCC employed thousands of young men to maintain, improve, and conserve state and federal lands. Approximately 4,000 CCC employees found themselves constructing visitor amenities and building many of the 800 miles (1,290 km) of trails and 384 miles (618 km) of roads that lace through Great Smoky Mountains National Park. The Smoky Mountains are some of the tallest peaks in the greater Appalachian Mountains chain, which runs from Maine to Georgia. They get their name from the "smoky" haze that hangs over the mountains; the Cherokee who originally settled here called them the Shaconage, or "place of blue smoke."

This contemporary poster was created to mark the 75th anniversary of the establishment of Great Smoky Mountains National Park. The attractive design features the John Cable gristmill amid fall foliage, calling attention to the park's rich southern Appalachian mountain heritage. The mill is one of more than 90 historic structures—gristmills, schools, churches, barns, and settlers' homes—that are found within the park.

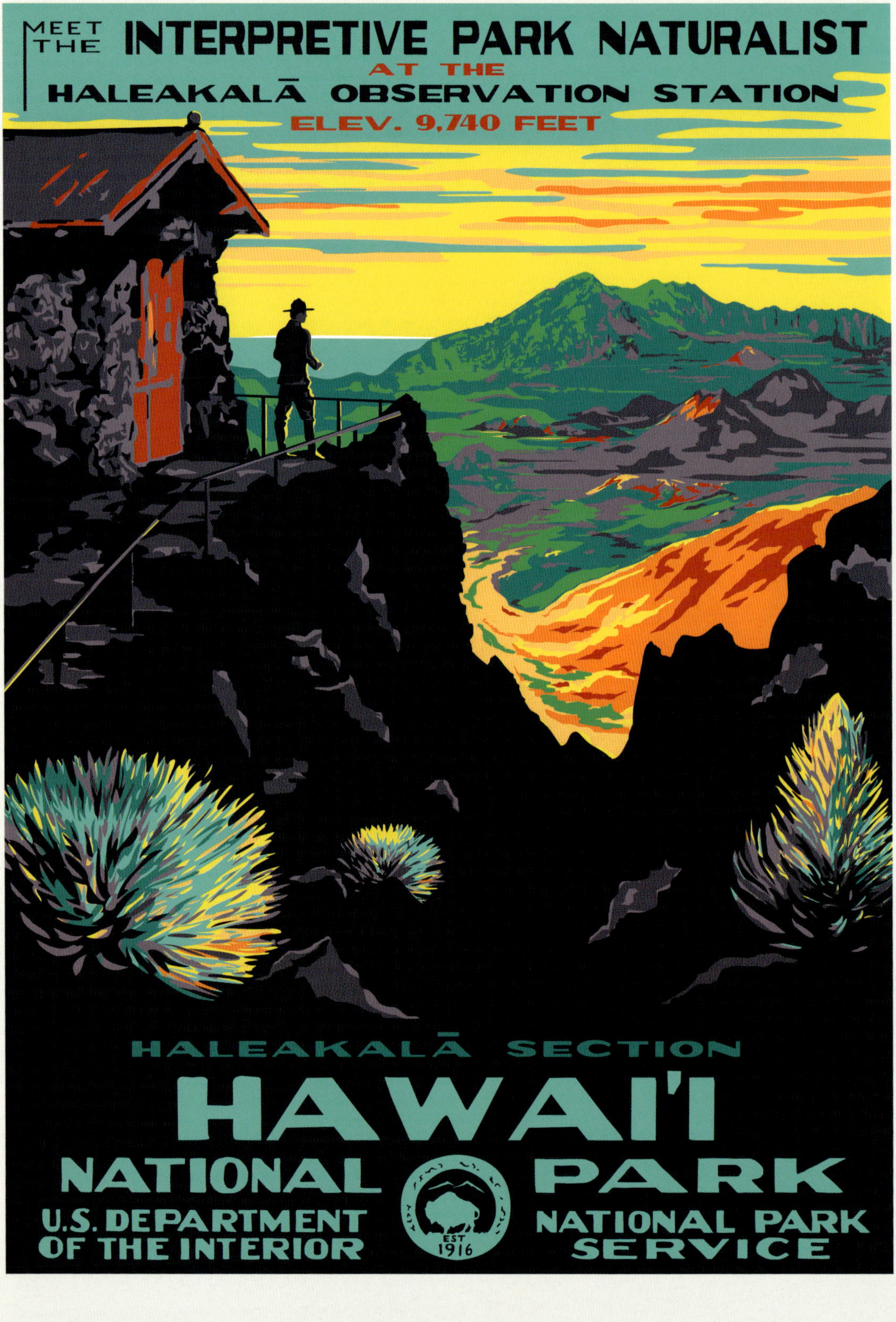

MEET THE
INTERPRETIVE PARK NATURALIST
AT THE
HALEAKALĀ OBSERVATION STATION
ELEV. 9,740 FEET
HALEAKALĀ SECTION
HAWAI'I
NATIONAL PARK
U.S. DEPARTMENT OF THE INTERIOR
EST 1916
NATIONAL PARK SERVICE

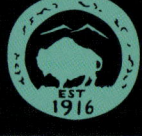

HALEAKALĀ N.P.

Maui, Hawaiian Islands
Est. July 1, 1961; 1916 (Hawai'i N.P.)
33,265 acres (13,461 ha)

Observe, be silent, and learn.
—Hawaiian Proverb

More than 2,000 miles (3,220 km) from the nearest continental landmass, the Hawaiian Archipelago is the most geographically isolated group of islands on Earth. Owing to its remoteness, over 90 percent of Hawaii's native flora and fauna are found nowhere else on earth, having evolved from species that most likely found their way over accidentally by air or sea. Haleakalā ("house of the sun") National Park, named for its resident dormant volcano, became a separate entity from Hawai'i National Park in 1961. The area is a smorgasbord of cultural history and natural wonders; in its diverse ecosystems from coastal to mountainous, desert to rain forest and much in between, it has more endangered species within its boundaries than any other site in the National Park System. The view from the summit is an astronomical sensation; a visit to the park is not complete without experiencing sunrise, sunset, or stargazing from what feels like the top of the world.

This poster, a contemporary design in 10 authentic colors, shows a historic scene. The individual depicted is an early Hawai'i National Park ranger—the first ranger was not assigned to the area until 1935—surveying the crater's features from the Haleakalā Observation Station, which was built by the Civilian Conservation Corps in 1936. Rosettes of silver pointed leaves of the Hawaiian silversword, native only to Maui, are seen in the foreground.

HAWAI'I VOLCANOES N.P.

Hawai'i (Big Island), Hawaiian Islands
Est. August 1, 1916
333,086 acres (134,795 ha)

For me its balmy airs are always blowing, its summer seas flashing in the sun; the pulsing of its surfbeat is in my ear; I can see its garlanded crags, its leaping cascades, its plumy palms drowsing by the shore.

—Mark Twain

Hawai'i Volcanoes National Park is home to two of the world's most active volcanoes: Kilauea and Mauna Loa. Due to a regular dose of volcanic activity, the Big Island of Hawai'i changes visibly everyday; Kilauea has been erupting since January 1983 and the resulting lava flow continues to reshape the landscape. Since 1983 alone, Kilauea's eruptions have added approximately 500 acres (200 ha) of new land to Hawai'i. Thrusting 4,190 feet (1,277 m) above sea level, Kilauea is actually dwarfed by its much larger but less volatile neighbor, Mauna Loa, which towers 13,677 feet (4,168 m) above the sea. The park supports unique native ecosystems, which has prompted its designation as an International Biosphere Reserve as well as a World Heritage Site. Visitors to the park can explore from sea to summit, where otherworldly geologic lava-made features coexist with forests in all stages of regrowth. Hawai'i Volcanoes National Park bears witness to the ever-evolving nature of our great planet Earth.

The Kilauea summit park poster is a contemporary design based on a 1924 slide depicting observers on the rim watching a major eruption in Kilauea's caldera. Within the summit caldera, the Halema'uma'u pit crater—the legendary home of Pele, the goddess of fire—remains an extremely unpredictable and explosive portion of the park.

JOSHUA TREE N.P.

California
Est. October 31, 1994; 1936 (N.M.)
792,623 acres (320,617 ha)

One time I saw a tiny Joshua tree sapling growing . . . I wanted to . . . replant it near our house. I told Mom that I would protect it from the wind and water it every day so that it could grow nice and tall and straight. Mom frowned at me. "You'd be destroying what makes it special," she said. "It's the Joshua tree's struggle that gives it its beauty."

—Jeannette Walls

The Joshua tree (*Yucca brevifolia*), the peculiar-looking evergreen that Mormon pioneers named for its resemblance to the biblical Joshua pointing the way to the Promised Land, inhabits the Mojave section, the "high desert," of so-named Joshua Tree National Park. The large branching yucca shares the sandy-plain terrain with giant granite rock formations. Below 3,000 feet (914 m), the park's alter-ego prevails, as the Colorado desert system fans across the park's eastern half, its "low desert" vegetation including creosote bushes, ocotillos, and chollas, which can tolerate the arid wilderness. Mercifully, five palm oases—out of a total of 158 throughout the U.S.—are found in Joshua Tree, areas of lush vegetation that provide welcome relief from what can be punishing conditions. A third, less-widespread ecosystem exists in the park's western region, where juniper and piñon pine grow in the Little San Bernardino Mountains.

This poster highlights Joshua trees, the park's signature plant species, against a backdrop of granite monoliths that permeate the landscape. The poster's title, created in the style of the WPA, reflects the park's original designation as a monument. Joshua Tree received national park status in 1994.

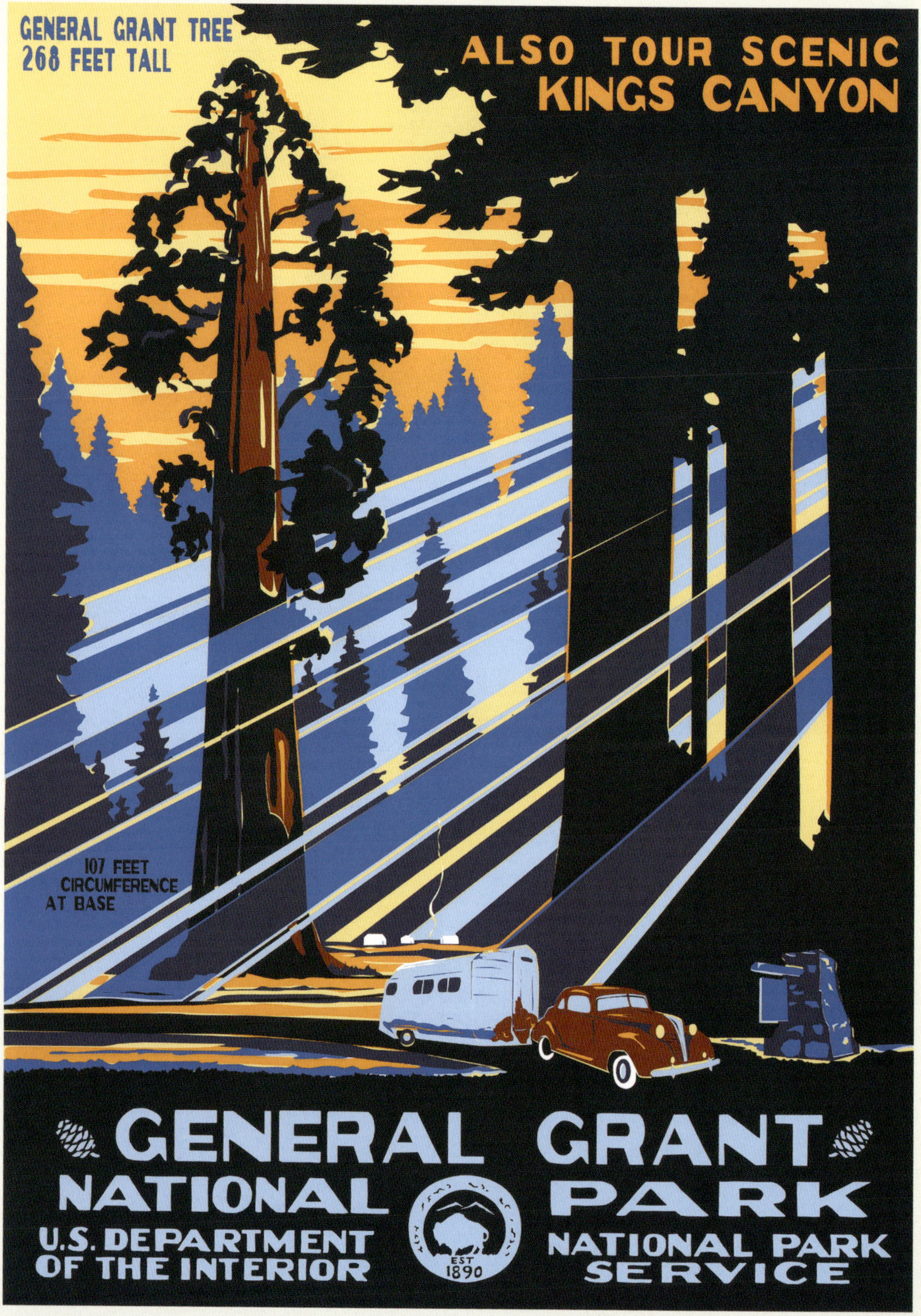
GENERAL GRANT TREE
268 FEET TALL
ALSO TOUR SCENIC
KINGS CANYON
107 FEET
CIRCUMFERENCE
AT BASE
GENERAL GRANT
NATIONAL PARK
U.S. DEPARTMENT
OF THE INTERIOR
EST
1890
NATIONAL PARK
SERVICE

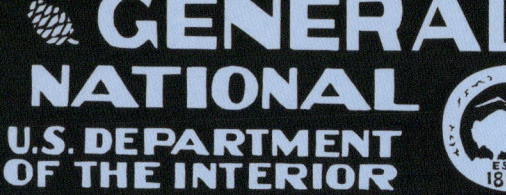

KINGS CANYON N.P.

Central California
Est. March 4, 1940; 1890 (General Grant N.P.)
461,901 acres (186,925 ha)

No nobler monuments of our love for beauty can be erected
than to preserve these oldest and biggest trees in the world
and these tallest trees in America.

—French Strother

General Grant National Park was established in 1890, one week after the establishment of Sequoia National Park—America's second national park—to protect and preserve the General Grant Grove of giant sequoia trees. General Grant National Park was absorbed into Kings Canyon National Park when the latter was established by Congress and President Franklin D. Roosevelt in 1940. Sequoia and Kings Canyon have been administered jointly by the National Park Service since World War II.

The centerpiece of Grant Grove is the General Grant Tree, which soars to a height of 267 feet (82 m), has a base circumference of 107.6 feet (32.8 m), and whose age is estimated at more than 1,650 years. The General Grant is the third tallest tree in the world, and the second tallest in the Grove. Named after Ulysses S. Grant, 18th President of the United States, this stately tree has been hailed as the "Nation's Christmas Tree" by President Calvin Coolidge and designated a "National Shrine" to all who have fallen in war by President Dwight D. Eisenhower.

Fitting indeed that the design for the contemporary serigraph print representing General Grant (Kings Canyon) National Park should feature the General Grant Tree, which along with its family of sequoias has been protected for over 120 years. Encouraging camping at the site, a 1937 Terraplane automobile pulling a Bowlus trailer is seen dwarfed by the towering landmark.

MESA VERDE N.P.

Colorado
Est. June 29, 1906
52,074 acres (21,074 ha)

*I had come upon the city of some extinct civilization, hidden
away in this inaccessible mesa for centuries, preserved in
the dry air and almost perpetual sunlight like a fly in amber,
guarded by the cliffs and the river and the desert.*

—Willa Cather

More than 600 cliff dwellings can be found in Colorado's Mesa
Verde National Park, including Cliff Palace (built c. 1200), an
astounding 150-room complex that housed approximately 100
Ancestral Puebloans (Anasazi) who called these canyons home for roughly
900 years. The exact reason that this flourishing culture abandoned the
site in the late 13th century is unknown—drought, warfare, and depletion
of natural resources are possibilities—but within just two generations, the
thriving community disappeared. Although local pioneers and prospectors
knew of the existence of the mesa-top Mesa Verde ruins as early as
the late 1700s, two ranchers accidentally stumbled upon the recessed
multi-storied Cliff Palace in 1888 while out searching for stray cattle. In
an effort to "preserve the works of man," today the park protects nearly
5,000 archaeological sites from the Ancestral Puebloan culture as well
as a wealth of natural resources. Due to its considerable archaeological
and cultural significance, Mesa Verde was also listed as a UNESCO World
Heritage Site in 1978.

This new poster design, created in the original WPA style, features
the remains of Square Tower House and the challenging terrain that defies
access to the cliff dwellings.

RANGER NATURALIST SERVICE
HEADQUARTERS PORT ANGELES

VISIT THE RANGER
STATIONS AT

DEER PARK
ELWHA
STORM KING
EAGLE
BOGACHIEL
HOH
QUINAULT
STAIRCASE

FOR INFORMATION ON

WILDERNESS TRAILS
COASTAL RAIN FORESTS
ROOSEVELT ELK
WILDFLOWER MEADOWS
WILDLIFE SANCTUARIES

FOOT AND SADDLE PARTIES WELCOME
ON 390 MILES OF TRAILS

OLYMPIC
NATIONAL  PARK

**U.S. DEPARTMENT
OF THE INTERIOR**

EST
1938

**NATIONAL PARK
SERVICE**

OLYMPIC N.P.

Washington
Est. June 29, 1938
922,651 acres (373,384 ha)

Keep [the service] youthful, vigorous, clean, and strong. We are not here to simply protect what we have been given so far; we are here to try to be the future guardians . . . as man and his industrial world expand and encroach on the last bastions of wilderness.

—Horace Albright, NPS Superintendent, 1929–33

Olympic National Park, on the Olympic Peninsula on the coast of Washington State, comprises three distinct ecosystems: subalpine forest and wildflower meadow; temperate forest; and Pacific shore. Such diverse climatic conditions support a wide variety of wildlife, from deer, elk, and bear that inhabit the meadows to raccoon, beaver, and mink in the lowlands, and salmon in the waterways. Whales, dolphins, and seals ply the Pacific waters offshore and more than 300 species of birds soar aloft. Notable are the endemic species such as the Olympic marmot and the Olympic snow mole that exist in this protected parkland and nowhere else on earth.

Olympic National Park covers an area that was not fully explored by Europeans until late in the 19th century, and its challenging terrain still presents significant obstacles to visitors, as 95 percent of the park is designated wilderness and no roads cross through its interior.

The park poster, a contemporary design in the style of the WPA, highlights the heart of Olympic National Park, where snow-capped peaks of the Olympic mountain range surrender to some of the best-preserved old-growth forest in the country. Here, a break in dense forest reveals a perspective from the north, across the Hoh River, with majestic Mount Olympus rising in the distance.

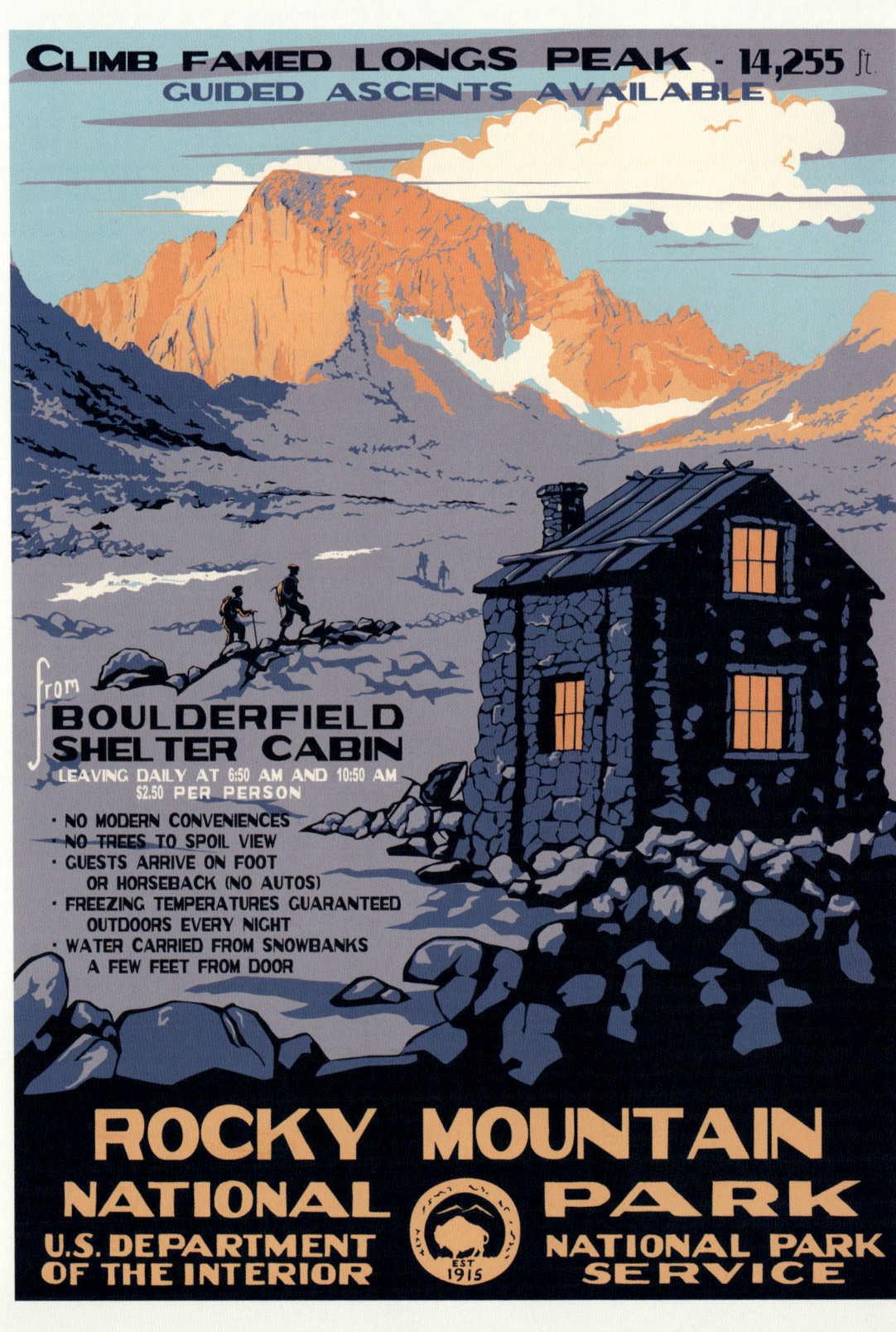

ROCKY MOUNTAIN N.P.

Colorado
Est. January 26, 1915
265,795 acres (107,563 ha)

*I come more and more to the conclusion that wilderness,
in America or anywhere else, is the only thing left that is
worth saving.*

—Edward Abbey

Amidst the backdrop of the Rocky Mountains, the rugged wilderness of Rocky Mountain National Park is home to a variety of ecosystems, including wetlands, montane, subalpine, and alpine. In this land of extremes, mirror-like lakes reflect hillsides of wildflower blooms only to give way to harsh, dry slopes at sky-high elevations seemingly devoid of plant or animal life. The park's 350 miles (563 km) of trails beckon hikers of all levels and abilities, offering moderate climbs on designated routes to challenging backcountry adventures. The park's signature Trail Ridge Road—with 11 of its 48 miles (18/77 km) winding above the treeline at over 11,500 feet (3,505 m)— was lauded by Parks Service director Horace Albright in 1931 before it was even built, and it has never disappointed.

The chosen design for the WPA-styled park poster features a silhouette of hikers crossing Boulder Field on their trek towards the summit. Longs Peak, at 14,259 feet (4,346 m), is the tallest peak in Rocky Mountain National Park and, not surprisingly, one of the park's most popular but difficult climbs. Boulderfield Cabin was chosen as the poster's featured historic structure after the cabin at Chasm Lake was destroyed by an avalanche. Boulderfield was built as a halfway house for climbers and was eventually condemned as the boulder field it was built upon was part of a glacier. Early park brochures provided the engaging phrases that accompany the poster's colorful, lively design.

SAGUARO N.P.

Arizona

Est. October 14, 1994; March 1, 1933 (N.M.)

91,445 acres (37,006 ha)

Desert beauty was "sublime" in the way that the romantic poets had used the word—not peaceful dales but rugged mountain faces, not reassuring but daunting nature, the earth's skin and haunches, its spines and angles arching prehistorically in sunlight.

—Julene Bair

Established to protect the nation's largest cacti, the saguaro (*Carnegiea gigantea*), Saguaro National Park's two districts bracket the east and west sides of the city of Tucson, Arizona. An icon of the Southwest, the slow-growing saguaro can grow to be 50 feet (15.2 m) tall and live for over 150 years; in the United States it is native only to the Sonoran Desert. More than just low-lying desert and cacti, the park supports extraordinary biodiversity within a small geographic area. The Rincon Mountain District east of Tucson spans in elevation from 2,500 feet (762 m) to 8,666 feet (2,641 m) at the summit of Mica Peak, and represents the plant and animal biodiversity equivalent of walking from Mexico to Canada. At the higher elevations, visitors may find black bears, white-tailed deer, Mexican spotted owls, Douglas fir, and aspen.

This new addition to the poster series collection features an impressive saguaro stand with the higher-elevation mountain district in the distance. The poster strays from the original poster series color palette in that the color scheme is brighter and more saturated than those used on the historic posters.

SEE AMERICA

COAST REDWOODS

WORLD'S TALLEST TREES

JEDEDIAH SMITH REDWOODS

DEL NORTE COAST REDWOODS

REDWOOD NATIONAL PARK

PRAIRIE CREEK REDWOODS

GRIZZLY CREEK REDWOODS

HUMBOLDT REDWOODS

RICHARDSON GROVE

MUIR WOODS NATIONAL MONUMENT

BIG BASIN REDWOODS

HENRY COWELL REDWOODS

PRAIRIE CREEK VISITOR CENTER

BUILT BY THE CCC IN 1933

REDWOODS

NATIONAL PARK SERVICE   CALIFORNIA STATE PARKS

REDWOOD NATIONAL & STATE PARKS

California

Est. October 2, 1968

131,983 acres (53,411 ha), in 4 parks: Redwood National Park, Del Norte Coast, Jedediah Smith, and Prairie Creek Redwoods State Parks

The redwoods, once seen, leave a mark or create a vision that stays with you always . . . It's not only their unbelievable stature, nor the color which seems to shift and vary under your eyes, no, they are not like any trees we know, they are ambassadors from another time.

—John Steinbeck

Prior to westward expansion and the discovery of gold in 1848, American Indians inhabited northern California's coastal rain forests. By the early 20th century, European-Americans had forced the Indians off their native lands, and 2,000,000 acres (809,000 ha) of towering ancient redwoods were nearly decimated by logging. Recognizing the potential loss of a national treasure—California's redwoods are the earth's tallest trees, and they can live for more than 2,000 years—the state of California began acquiring redwood groves and protecting them within state parks. As part of FDR's New Deal, the Civilian Conservation Corps was instrumental in improving access to and amenities in California's state parks. When Redwood National Park was established in 1968, it encompassed three of those state parks. Today, only 5 percent of the original old-growth forests remain, but the remnants of logging are slowly being erased, restoration continues, and the redwood habitat continues to thrive.

This vintage-inspired poster uses a "window" design to emphasize the vastness of a redwood grove in California's Prairie Creek (under the auspices of the National and State Park systems), paying special homage to the Prairie Creek Visitor Center built by the CCC in 1933.

SEE GIANT SEQUOIAS
AND THE GENERAL SHERMAN TREE ** THE WORLD'S LARGEST

274 FEET
TALL

102 FEET
CIRCUMFERENCE
AT BASE

SEQUOIA
NATIONAL ✹ PARK
U.S. DEPARTMENT
OF THE INTERIOR
EST
1916
NATIONAL PARK
SERVICE

SEQUOIA N.P.

California
Est. September 25, 1890
404,064 acres (163,519 ha)

What is the purpose of the giant sequoia tree? The purpose of
the giant sequoia tree is to provide shade for the tiny titmouse.

—Edward Abbey

Sequoia, in the southern Sierra Nevada range, was initially established to protect Giant Forest—one of the largest sequoia groves— from logging. However, as visitors began arriving to the area, development—roads, camping facilities, cabins—began to have a negative impact on the forest's resources. Early recognition of this problem restored much of the forest's integrity and prevented future development. With the distinction of being America's second national park, Sequoia was subsequently aligned with the contiguous lands of Kings Canyon National Park, sharing both borders and BIG attractions: trees, mountains, and canyons, and hundreds of miles of trails that lead visitors to the park's abundant natural features. Mount Whitney, the highest summit in the 48 contiguous states, is located within the park, as is the General Sherman Tree, the largest tree (by volume) in the world. Panoramic views of the park can be had from atop Moro Rock, a granite dome that is accessed by 400 stairs built into the monolith by the CCC.

Intended to complement the General Grant poster, both designs feature stately sequoias and the arrival of visitors by car and camper. The Sequoia National Park design shows a 1940 "woodie" pulling a teardrop trailer through the giant forest. The General Sherman tree, with its massive circumference noted, dwarfs the tiny silhouettes of inspired onlookers at its base in the tranquil grove.

SHENANDOAH N.P.

Virginia
Est. December 26, 1935
197,411 acres (79,889 ha)

If you drive to, say, Shenandoah National Park, or the Great Smoky Mountains, you'll get some appreciation for the scale and beauty of the outdoors. When you walk into it, then you see it in a completely different way. You discover it in a much slower, more majestic sort of way.

—Bill Bryson

With matchless beauty and seemingly infinite resources, the Blue Ridge Mountains and the surrounding valleys that comprise Shenandoah National Park provide a refreshing escape from the everyday bustle. The park boasts stunning natural features, from its dense interior—95 percent of the park is treed—and numerous waterfalls to its breathtaking panoramas and 500 miles (805 km) of trails (including 101 miles/162 km of the Appalachian Trail). Overlooks along Skyline Drive afford the opportunity to stop and behold the scenic splendor of the Appalachian Blue Ridge, and provide access to trailheads for those adventurous souls who want to explore the paths less traveled.

The park supports a wide variety of flora and fauna. Besides forests rich in pine, oak, hickory, maple, birch, ash, basswood, and blackgum, flowering shrubs and seasonal wildflowers deck the land. Wildlife, from black bears and white-tailed deer to salamanders—the Appalachian Mountains are known for this amphibian's diverse population—move freely.

In a tribute to Shenandoah's clear mountain streams and ancient geologic history, this contemporary poster features the iconic waterfalls of Whiteoak Canyon.

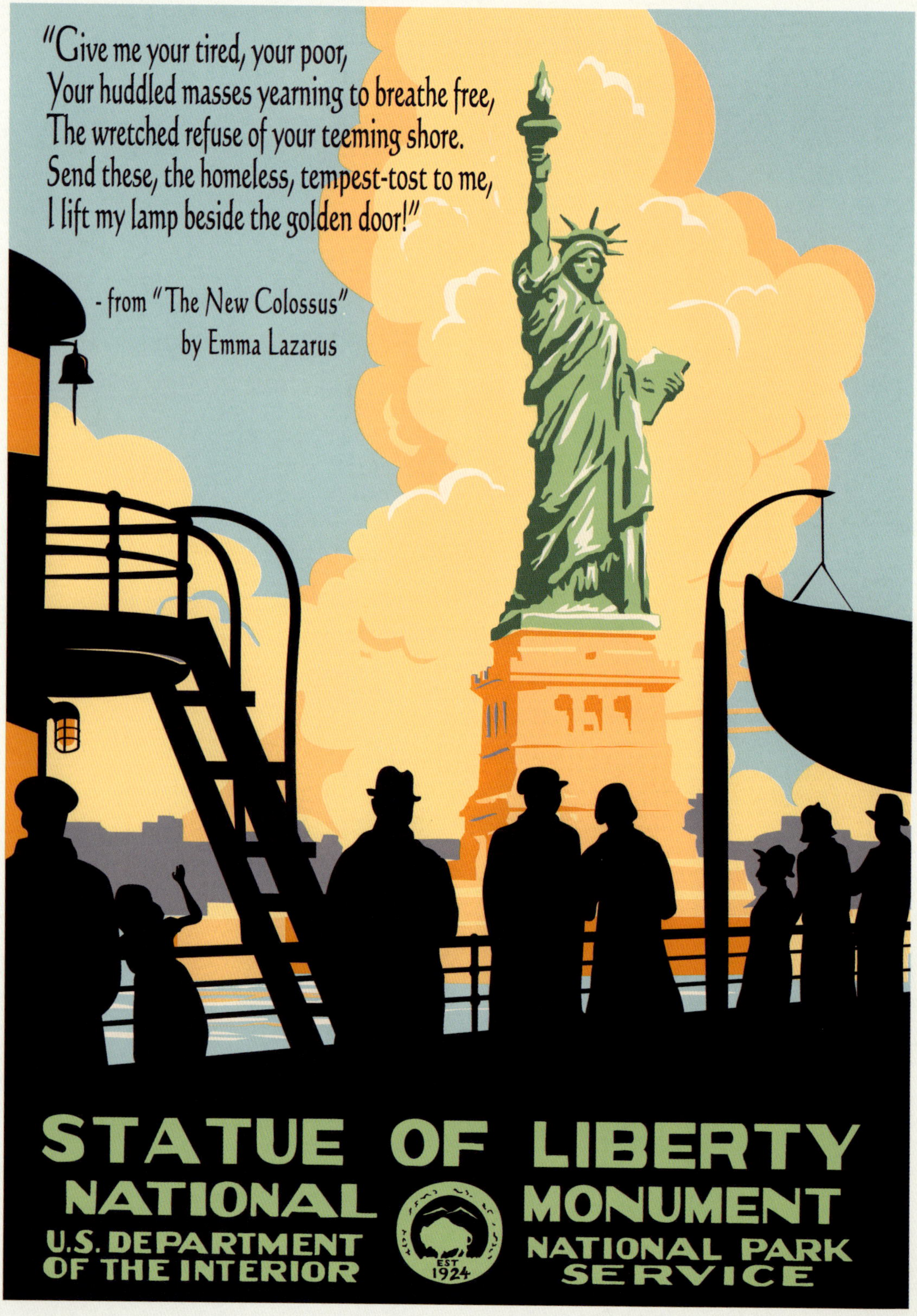

"Give me your tired, your poor,
Your huddled masses yearning to breathe free,
The wretched refuse of your teeming shore.
Send these, the homeless, tempest-tost to me,
I lift my lamp beside the golden door!"

- from "The New Colossus"
  by Emma Lazarus

STATUE OF LIBERTY
NATIONAL MONUMENT
U.S. DEPARTMENT OF THE INTERIOR
NATIONAL PARK SERVICE

EST 1924

STATUE OF LIBERTY N.M.

Liberty Island, New York
Est. October 15, 1924 (N.M.), Opened October 28, 1886
3.3 acres (1.3 ha)

*This nation has placed its destiny in the hands and heads
and hearts of millions of free men and women; and its faith
in freedom under the guidance of God. Freedom means the
supremacy of human rights everywhere . . . Our strength is
our unity of purpose.*

—President Franklin D. Roosevelt

Since 1886 Lady Liberty has welcomed the huddled masses to America, a symbol of freedom and a vision of hope for the millions of immigrants entering New York Harbor in search of a new life. The statue was given to the United States as a gesture of friendship by France, who supported the colonies in the American Revolution and admired their building of a successful democratic nation. Designed by sculptor Frédéric-Auguste Bartholdi, this 305-foot (93 m) copper-clad monument is supported by a steel frame engineered by Alexandre-Gustave Eiffel, of Eiffel Tower fame. It was constructed in France, shipped to the U.S. in multiple pieces, and assembled on Liberty Island (then Bedloe's Island). On October 28, 1886, "Liberty Enlightening the World" was unveiled to New Yorkers with great fanfare, and became an icon for the American immigration experience.

Depicting Bartholdi's intent to have every ship entering New York Harbor pass by Lady Liberty, this poster—a new design in the WPA style—uses silhouette to illustrate the countless nameless immigrants who relied on her message as they arrived in the land of opportunity. The famous poem by Emma Lazarus, featured in the design, is inscribed on a plaque in the statue's pedestal.

U.S. DEPARTMENT OF THE INTERIOR

Washington, D.C.

Est. March 3, 1849

Manages 507 million acres (205,000,000 ha)

As I view this serviceable new structure I like to think of it as symbolical of the Nation's vast resources that we are sworn to protect, and this stone that I am about to lay, as the cornerstone of a conservation policy that will guarantee to future Americans the richness of their heritage.

—President Franklin D. Roosevelt,
dedication of the DOI building, April 16, 1936

Built in record time between April 1935 and December 1936, the Department of the Interior headquarters was the first building constructed in the nation's capital during President Franklin D. Roosevelt's administration. It was considered state-of-the-art with numerous modern conveniences, and with one percent of the construction budget set aside for artwork, it features more New Deal–era murals than any other federal building. The street address—1849 C Street—is deliberate, as it pays tribute to the year the Department was created. Today, the building is home to the Secretary of the Interior and more than 2,000 of the Department's 70,000 employees.

This poster commemorates the 75th anniversary of the Interior Museum, which opened within the headquarters in 1938. The museum featured this design in its 2014–15 retrospective exhibition, POSTERity, which included six original WPA national park posters as well as a full complement of the contemporary screen printed editions.

NATIONAL PARK AND WPA POSTER RESOURCES

U.S. Department of the Interior
1849 C Street, NW
Washington DC 20240
Phone: (202) 208-3100
doi.gov

National Park Service
1849 C Street NW
Washington DC 20240
nps.gov
asknps@nps.gov

Library of Congress
Thomas Jefferson Building
10 First Street SE
Washington DC 20540
Phone: (202) 707-8000
loc.gov/pictures
loc.gov/rr/askalib/

Library of Congress Work Projects Administration (WPA) Poster Collection
loc.gov/pictures/collection/wpapos/

The National Archives and Records Administration
8601 Adelphi Road
College Park MD 20740-6001
Phone: (866) 272-6272
archives.gov

Ranger Doug's Enterprises
2442 NW Market Street #567
Seattle WA 98107
Phone: (888) WPA POSTers (888-972-7678)
rangerdoug.com

THE SEARCH CONTINUES . . .

The Great Smoky Mountains and Wind Cave posters remain undiscovered.
If you happen to come upon any original WPA National Parks posters, please call
the National Park Service at 202-208-6843 or Doug Leen at 888-972-7678.